Praise for question
method

"[W]ith its unreliable, unnamed narrator and twisted turns, and taking cues from classic noir and devil-at-the-crossroad blues, the novel is one long blast of existential despair ... the ill wind whipping through these pages leaves its mark."
— *Kirkus Reviews*

"In *Thirteen Question Method*, David L. Ulin brings out the chiaroscuro of Los Angeles, the brightness of its glamour contrasted with the deep shadows of its sordidness. You can feel the heat rise from the sidewalks as it does from this book, until the moment everything explodes. By then, Ulin has expertly guided the reader through the streets and then into the canyons, ultimately taking us into the deepest abyss of all—the human soul. It's hot there, but also cold. That strange and frightening paradox is all too typical of the city, and Ulin makes sure we will never forget it with this indelible novel. No one knows Los Angeles, or noir, quite like he does."
— **Viet Thanh Nguyen**, author of *The Sympathizer*

"Spare, brutal, and laced with the dark, dizzying smoke of California wildfire, *Thirteen Question Method* is a hot shot of Los Angeles noir from one of our city's finest writers."
— **Steph Cha**, author of *Your House Will Pay*

"There hasn't been a Los Angeles noir novel as dark-hearted as David L. Ulin's *Thirteen Question Method* since Charles Willeford's *The Woman Chaser*. Go ahead and rewrite the canon and put Ulin's first crime novel on the top of the list – this is fast, sexy, weird, and completely unhinged. You'll read it quickly and then you'll read it again, just to make sure you didn't miss a single word. An instant classic."
— **Tod Goldberg**, *New York Times* bestselling author of *The Low Desert* and the *Gangsterland* trilogy

"This is either Josef K in a Raymond Chandler plot, or Boethius caught like Vincent Price in the most Los Angeles story there is. Either way, this one grabs you by the face and drags you through the forest dark, which turns out to be more familiar than you want."
— **Stephen Graham Jones**, author of *The Only Good Indians*

"A masterclass in noir that both honors and elevates the genre, *Thirteen Question Method* is in a category of its own. Ulin's novel is sharp, nasty, and unsettling in all the best ways."
— **Ivy Pochoda**, author of *Sing Her Down, These Women, Wonder Valley,* and *Visitation Street*

"I haven't read a book as incendiary, relentless, and downright sinister as *Thirteen Question Method*. With this novel, David L. Ulin joins the ranks of crime fiction heavyweights like Raymond Chandler, James M. Cain, and Patricia Highsmith. The voice is stylish and sexy, full of jagged edges and liquid smooth curves that will leave readers holding their breath until the very end. A lesson in how to write noir and all the deliciously disturbing things that come with it."
— **Alex Espinoza**, author of *Still Water Saints* and *Cruising: An Intimate History of a Radical Pastime*

"David L Ulin's *Thirteen Question Method* is a smart shot of a crime novel — so intelligent, so creepy, so noir. The anxieties of every character (including the great city of Los Angeles) burn off the pages in this ode to the worst of us."
— **Rachel Howzell Hall**, *New York Times* and *Wall Street Journal* bestselling novelist

a novel

thirteen question method

david l. ulin

Outpost19 | San Francisco
outpost19.com

Ulin, David L.
Thirteen Question Method / David L. Ulin

ISBN: 9781944853907

Available in paperback and ebook editions.

OUTPOST19

ORIGINAL PROVOCATIVE READING
SAN FRANCISCO | @OUTPOST19

thirteen question method

david l. ulin

For Mark Haskell Smith

The thirteen question method is the one to use.

— Chuck Berry

QUESTION NUMBER ONE:
DO YOU WANT TO HAVE FUN?

The woman across the courtyard was screaming. Ribbons of raving like a coyote's wail. I was in the living room when it started, feet curled beneath me on the sofa. For an instant, her voice sounded predatory, and my heart jolted with adrenaline as if I might be the prey. Then I recognized the modulations, intonations, that elaborate ebb and flow.

It was a Saturday night in late July and the weather had felt tropical for days. Muggy, sultry, heat rising from the pavement in shimmering waves. Out in the canyons, wildfires scorched the dry brush. Control was a word from another lexicon. People say fall is fire season in Southern California, but I think of summer as the meanest time. Tonight, however, the air was clear and I'd had the windows open. Now, I got off the couch and went around the room, closing myself in. I switched on some music. The problem with the woman wasn't that she was screaming, it was that I had heard it before.

I knew who she was. Sort of. Which is to say I recognized her face. Angular yet also moon-shaped — a different look each time she caught my eye. Hair just below the shoulders, brown with fading streaks of blue. She lived alone, in the unit across the courtyard. Mid-thirties, just a couple of years younger than I was. Slender but full-hipped, a little swagger, stylish in her skinny jeans and ankle boots.

I noticed stuff like that, especially the boots …

It would be a stretch to say she noticed me.

No, that's not right, I'm sure she'd noticed, in the way we have of noticing people we don't particularly care about or know. I was just a guy living in another unit, nondescript, going prematurely gray. I had moved here after the implosion of my marriage, in the slipstream of that assault. I had been looking … not for a home, nor for any feeling of belonging, just for a place that I might land.

This apartment was the first I'd looked at: one bedroom, a living room with a kitchen on the other side of a half-wall, counter, a couple of stools. I bought all the furniture — couch, bed, chair, coffee table — in a single afternoon. I just wanted it dealt with, didn't want to have it weigh on me.

In the final weeks, or months, that had been how I felt about the marriage also; I just wanted it to be finished, whatever it was. Should I stay or should I go, like the old Clash song, which I remembered listening to a lot the year I turned twenty, a couple of decades after its release. I was just starting with the woman who would become my wife. Now, that part of my life was finished. In this apartment I was waiting, waiting for a future that would never come.

The music growling through my speakers was of an earlier vintage: Little Walter, Memphis Minnie, Bessie Smith. My wife used to chide me for living in the past. *Why don't you listen to music from this century?* she would ask, not always kindly, but the truth was that I wanted to be reassured. Old music didn't hold surprises; I knew every riff, every note and flutter. Old music didn't knock me off my stride, didn't need to be assessed or figured out. Old music came with its own, familiar associations, as fully formed as memories.

This could be a mixed blessing, as when a recording like Howlin' Wolf's "How Many More Years" came up in the mix, as it did now. That was a song I used to belt out in the car, thinking about my wife, angry tears, the product of some projection, building up behind my eyes. This is the other thing about old music, that it encodes our memories, the couldadones and shouldadones, the lines we once believed spoke to our souls. *How many more years* … what a fucking joke. We couldn't even keep our wedding vows.

And yet, what did I expect? It wasn't just her, it was me also, and anyway the point of the song was not about loving someone, it was about how it feels to be unloved. Maybe that was why I responded to it, because it allowed me, when I sang along, to imagine myself into that cycle of regret and recrimination, the way the singer is always singing to himself. As for my wife, ex-wife, well … she didn't exactly figure into that equation. With her, there had been no regret, no recrimination, no *waiting*.

One day it was over, and *we* were done.

Whatever, old news, water under the bridge. Another aspect of my life I could not control. The song came to an end, as they always do, and in the sudden silence, I was aware of a deeper silence: the woman across the courtyard had stopped her screaming, had ceased to make any noise at all. The air in my living room was still and close, as if a blanket had been dropped over the night. I could feel sweat bead in my armpits, at the base of my back. I felt a little dizzy as I drifted toward the windows, thinking I might open them again. Before I could work the slide on the first one, I became aware of a scuffling sound, as if a small animal were burrowing or hiding; as I stood there, it resolved into a quiet knocking at my door.

I looked at the clock — nine thirty. Crossing the room felt like wading through a swamp. Suddenly I became aware of an exhaustion so deep it was all I could do to remain upright. I took a step and then another one, that knocking in the background like a blinking pulse. At the door, I drew a deep breath, ran my fingers through my hair. I knew who it was without even asking, no need to look through the peephole, and sure enough, once I turned the latch, it was she who was revealed. The woman from across the courtyard, two-tone hair hanging in front of her eyes like a cowl, a mask, some form of protection, as if she were hiding in plain sight.

She was pretty, that was the first thing. I had never seen her up close, or not up close *enough*, had never noticed the lavender that flecked her hazel eyes, and her lids were ringed with kohl. Her hand was raised, fingers arranged into a loose fist, as if I had caught her in the middle of a knock. She wore black nail polish, chipped and frayed.

"Hello," I said. "Can I help you?"

"I" … she answered, and her voice trailed off, as if

3

she had not spoken at all.

In the distance, a siren, police or ambulance or fire truck, dopplered its careening wail against the hills. The building was in Hollywood, on the south side of Franklin, just below the Magic Castle. Not long after I moved in, there had been a pandemic of car fires in the neighborhood. One night, twenty-one, the next eighteen, and each time I heard a siren now, it brought back those desperate hours, cruisers crisscrossing the neighborhood, a sky that stank of kerosene, or lighter fluid. The guy the cops arrested said he didn't do it, but he'd been through some shit, a breakup, the loss of a loved one, I can't remember anymore. Eventually he walked, and disappeared back into the city as if he'd never emerged from it at all.

The woman from across the courtyard didn't meet my gaze.

"You live across the way, right?" I asked, waving in the direction of her apartment. She nodded but still she wouldn't look at me. "Is there something" … I went on, and now she glanced up and shook her head sharply, eyes glinting in the light from the living room. "Do you want to come in?" I said.

Inside the apartment, she peered around like a wary animal before turning to me. "I want to apologize," she started, voice flat and liquid, with a throaty rasp. I gave her a look as if I didn't know what she meant; she raised her eyebrows and threw the same look back at me. "I know you heard me," she continued. "I saw your windows go down. I couldn't help it. Don't you ever need to scream?"

Ever need to scream? My whole life felt that way, but how could I explain that to someone I'd just met? Anyway, what about last week, or the week before? This was not a one-time thing, after all.

I felt paralyzed, as if I could stay in this room, this position, forever. The fires would arrive, or the hills would come pouring down in an earthquake or a mudslide, and they'd find us, still standing here before the door. It would look like something, like we'd been together, but it wouldn't be. Just two separate lives, in parallel. How could they know that we had only met this moment, that we had exchanged barely a dozen words before the walls came tumbling down?

And yet, what if all that chaos, that cacophony, led not to devastation but to escape, an unexpected freedom? What if it could set us free? Like the old spiritual promised: *My dungeon shook and my chains fell off.*

That was what I wanted to happen to me.

The music switched to Elmore James, "The Sky is Crying," another kind of spiritual. At the first sharp bite of slide guitar, her mouth curled into something like a grin. I had no idea what we were doing, but it felt as if some common ground had been afforded, as if some accommodation had been reached.

"Why don't you sit down?" I said. And then: "I don't like to scream."

"One of those, huh? Prefer to keep it bottled up."

"I'm not bottled up."

"Not much. You couldn't get those windows down fast enough."

"If you were so worked up, what were you doing looking at my windows? I could get the wrong idea, you know. Think the whole screaming thing was ... I don't know ... an act."

"It's not an act, let me assure you. But thanks for your concern."

"Hey," I said. "Don't take this the wrong way, but you came over here."

For a moment, she didn't say anything. Then, slowly, she began to laugh. The sound was not unlike her shrieking: percolating, building as it rose. I could hear a whisper of disturbance underneath it, could imagine it slipping the bonds of restraint. She moved further into the apartment, rubbing her eyes with the heel of her hand.

"What does a girl have to do to get a drink around here?" she asked, and as she did, I understood that I had been right all along, that whatever else was happening in this moment, she was also playing a part.

I went to the cabinet and pulled out a bottle: Maker's Mark. I was a man of simple pleasures; when I drank, it was bourbon. No frills. Not that I was a drinker especially, although that depends on how you define *especially*. Since I wasn't working, the witching hour had gotten earlier and earlier, from six to five to four thirty, although that didn't happen every day. I'd been trying to take it easy this evening. I'd been imagining what it might be like to be productive, although how to make that happen I couldn't see. I was tired, with a slight paunch around my middle. When I thought about where I might be going, it was hard to imagine a world bigger than this room.

I brought out glasses, ice, set it all on the coffee table, a sad and small display. She smiled again, lips curled into something like a question mark, as if she weren't sure that she should stay. Then she dropped a couple of ice cubes in a tumbler and dumped a healthy pour of Maker's over the top.

"Aren't you going to have one?" she asked, but I still wasn't sure, so after waiting for a bunch of seconds she raised her glass to me and took a long pull from the drink.

And I knew I should say something, but really what was there to say? Here we were, in my apartment, two strangers brought together by proximity, not a thing in common but the fact that we each lived in the same bungalow court. All I knew about her was that she was a screamer. That was nothing, or maybe everything. Either way, now that she was sitting here, it might be a good idea to find out.

"That wasn't the first time I heard you screaming," I said, my voice flat and measured as a metronome.

"No."

"You want to tell me what's been happening?"

"I don't know."

She looked at me, eyes hooded; I gave in and poured a drink. Just a finger or two in the bottom of the glass, neat, although there was nothing neat about this.

"You don't need to apologize," I said, or maybe

I just thought it — either way, something opened up. She took another sip of whiskey and started speaking, words like the low hum of mosquitoes, hard to make out and yet clear at once.

"My father died," she said.

"I'm sorry."

"It happened a few months ago." She spilled a bit more whiskey into her glass, drank again, as if gathering strength. "I didn't like him." She looked up at me, gauging my reaction. "What I mean is: we weren't close."

I knew what she was saying; I had felt the same about my parents, although I didn't mention that. I didn't react, just sat and waited, trying to remain neutral, as if I weren't here.

"He left me a bunch of money," she went on, "but his wife is contesting the will."

Money? I thought. But all I said was: "Your mother?"

"No, she's dead too. Died when I was fifteen. I'm talking about his second wife."

"That must be complicated," I said, keeping my voice flat, holding my gaze to her eyes.

"Complicated doesn't begin to describe it. She says that she deserves it all. She says he was having the will rewritten, that he planned to cut me out. She has her lawyer say this, then she calls and tells me too. That's when the screaming starts."

She grinned at me, her eyes dark, lips lopsided, just this side of sloppy. I felt desire flicker like a flame. It began in the center of my stomach, then rose in a flush through my chest and out across my fingers, like some sort of electricity or rash. It had been so long since I'd been with anyone. The last time with my wife had been a fiasco in every sort of way. Now here she was, the woman from across the courtyard, two feet away from me in my own living room, the smell of her perfume — floral, light, just below the level of conscious reckoning — filling the air between us like a siren song. She was looking at me as if waiting for a reaction. She was looking at me as if this

7

were a test. *Why are you telling me this?* I wanted to ask, but then I had a … I don't know what you'd call it, not quite a premonition but a warning. *Don't*, I thought, *don't do it.* "I don't even know your name," I said.

She laughed again then, the sound light but tinged with something, a breath of wistfulness, or maybe of despair. "Corrina," she answered, "like the old Bob Wills song."

Bob Wills? That hadn't been what I was expecting. It was like seeing her in another light. I knew that recording; I had listened to it many times. For a moment, I thought I might play it to show her, but just as quickly I decided to leave it be.

Meanwhile, through the speakers, Elmore James had given way to Robert Johnson. "Kind Hearted Woman" … I listened for a moment to the low moan of his singing, the steady plink of his guitar. This song had been recorded in a hotel room, not long before Johnson died of syphilis or was poisoned by a lover's jealous boyfriend or Satan showed up at the crossroads to claim his soul. All of it lost now in the mist of history or myth. I had never liked the crossroads story, not because I didn't believe in the Devil — although I didn't — but because it didn't give Johnson enough agency. It made him a passive recipient of his own fate.

Selling your soul was too easy. Life was not so simple as that.

"So what are you going to do, Corrina?" I asked, as if we had known each other for a long time, as if we were old friends. The question sat there, on the table between us, with the ice and glasses, like something to be shared.

"I don't know," she said. "I suppose I could always kill her. Or have her killed." She stopped, looked right at me, eyes as clear as running water. Then she raised her glass in a sloppy toast, or a salute.

And maybe I should have spoken then. No: no maybes at all. But there was something in the room between us, something more than silence, as if a gauntlet had been thrown. I knew enough not to take it serious-ly; we didn't know each other, and I guessed she'd been drinking, or maybe drugging, since before she arrived. But there are moments when what you say or don't say matters, and this felt like one of them. *Are you kidding? You must be kidding.* This was something I could say. Or: *That's not funny, even as a joke.* As the moment extended, however, the opportunity to fill it faded, and all I was left with was my complicity.

Complicity? Yes, for not changing the direction, for not changing the collective mind. Instead, my inability or unwillingness to respond gave shape to the moment, and turned it into something different than what it had been, something she and I now shared.

Not that I thought anything would come of it; she didn't seem that kind. She was just talking, voicing her frustration, we were responsible individuals, after all. We were sitting in my living room on a Saturday night, having a few drinks, like people everywhere in town. I waved the Maker's in her direction, offering another belt. As I filled her glass, I imagined how it might go, not the killing but the rest. Up close, the jeans she was wearing were contoured and tight. She was in a thin blouse over a pale tank top, close to the color of her flesh. If I squint-ed, I could almost picture her without it, almost picture moving to the bedroom, removing every stitch except her boots. I could almost picture her hair hanging across my face as her body rose and fell. Almost, almost, almost … I could almost see it, but something, I couldn't quite put a finger on it, held me back. I kept thinking about her skin, so smooth across the jawline. It had been a long time since I'd touched a woman there.

Then she lurched, or belched, a disruption in the corner of my eye. The image, never fully rendered, faded, and I was back in my living room.

"Bathroom?" she asked, and before I could an-swer, she was moving, as if she had been here before. She had, of course, in a manner of speaking; these units were all laid out the same. As I watched, she lurched again, unsteady, careened across the room. Through the bathroom door, I could hear her retching. It was like the churning of an engine, sputtering and catching, sputtering again. I wanted to help, to hold her hair if nothing else, but that felt unbearably intimate. It had been less than an hour since she'd shown up at my door.

There is a line between imagination and reality, between what we wish for and who we are. What she had said sat on one side of that line, as did everything that I'd been thinking; there was no way either of those things were going to happen, not tonight or any other night.

That was where I was now, in some sort of nether region, neither intimate nor distant, in which I knew too much about her and also not enough. She had not asked anything about me, nor would she, I realized as she emerged from the bathroom, wobbling a little, hair damp and kohl streaked beneath her reddened eyes. That was fine; there was nothing I wanted her to know. I was just waiting, occupying this space, this landscape, biding time. One instant, one set of actions, was as meaningless as the next. Regardless of what happened, I'd wake up tomorrow and it would be Sunday, and I'd be faced with the gaping emptiness of everything. Nothing to do and all the time in the world to do it, until time telescoped and folded in on itself, like the implosion of a supernova into a black hole.

"I'm sorry," she said. "I should go." And then: "I cleaned up the bathroom as best I could."

"Don't worry about it. Happens to everyone," I told her, although the truth was that I didn't want to know.

She stood still for a moment, as if she were considering. Then she appeared to make up her mind. "What I said before?" she began, her voice pitched halfway between a statement and a question. "You know I wasn't serious, right?"

"What you said before?" I asked, as if not remembering, until she gave me that raised-eyebrow look again. "All right," I said. "I'll keep it in mind."

"Sometimes I just say shit. I don't even mean it."

10

I nodded, but there was a part of me that could still hear her screaming in the night.

"Anyway," she went on, "I appreciate your hospitality. Maybe we can do it again sometime."

I watched her weave a little to the door, any desire I might have thought I felt now dissipated and remote. The door opened and closed like a portal to another world. I was alone again, the only evidence that she had been here the empty tumbler on the table and whatever was waiting for me in the bathroom. I sat still for a moment, as if reconstituting, then headed into the kitchen for the mop.

The bathroom wasn't bad, although it smelled: slightly bitter, slightly sweet. I hit the switch, turned on the fan, the whir of that tiny engine cutting a passage through the silence of the night. She had made an effort, I had to give her that; the floor and the toilet were clean. In the middle of the room, my bath towel lay crumpled, damp, streaked with something that looked like chocolate, or mud.

I went back to the kitchen, got a garbage bag, bundled the towel into it. Briefly, I thought about dropping it in the hamper, but I didn't want that mixed in with my clothes. I left it while I mopped the floor again and wiped down all the surfaces with Lysol. The odor lingered, although it was growing fainter, cut with the antiseptic cleanser smells.

When I was done, I took the garbage bag and stepped out to the courtyard, making my way to the back gate where the dumpster was. Above the safety lights, the sky was hooded, wrapped in gauze. The heat felt close and itchy, and I couldn't catch my breath. Somewhere, I could whiff the scent of smoke, of flame, like a subtle undertone. Somewhere, I could make out the soft sound of a guitar, but it was too low to recognize. *Why don't you listen to music from this century?* ... no, that was all behind me now.

I let go of the garbage bag and closed the dumpster, stashing it like a piece of evidence. Then I returned to my apartment, washed my hands, and fixed myself a drink. Taking it easy — one more decision that I had apparently let go. The Maker's burned a little going down, but the sensation faded, and I finished the drink while I was standing, poured another one.

On the stereo, Howlin' Wolf was back, rumbling that he was a back door man. I remembered the first time I had heard the song, the Doors cover, the strange titillation to hear someone singing about that. It was all over the blues, these double entendres, coded messages, I want to call them, although the code was right in front of you, ridiculously easy to crack. *Wang dang doodle; squeeze my lemon till the juice runs down my leg.* It had been this that drew me first to the music, the sense that it was both transgressive and of the every day. What we all wanted, a little bit of connection, the hit and run of it, consolation for the loneliness of being alive. I'd had it with my wife or something like it, until it all went sour. That last time we'd been together, my lemon ripe and sticky, her honeypot, her thistle pie. Now I was alone, left with nothing but memories. And those memories … less a consolation than a series of rebukes. What had happened? I knew what had happened, but I didn't want to go there. Just another lost opportunity, something else that did not work out. Like the woman tonight, her unexpected arrival, and the equally unexpected way she disappeared.

I didn't want to listen to a song about fucking; it would only make me remember what I had lost. So I clicked through the playlist until I heard the rising of another record, Chuck Berry's "Thirteen Question Method."

What a strange track it was, so weird, so unexpected, neither rocker, exactly, nor ballad, existing in the liminal space between. I had always had a soft spot for this one: a song built on questions, a series of suppositions, a call rather than a response. Maybe it was that slack-key guitar playing, so distinct from Berry's signature sound. Back when he was still willing to try something different, before he fell into the routine of expectation, before music became straitjacket more than art. Maybe it was those lyrics, so open and so yearning, offering not a story but a poem. Everything was possible, that was the implicit promise, and it made me hopeful, even though I understood it was a lie.

After the song was over, I turned off the music, opened the windows to the night. There was no difference between the air inside and out, both were thick and still and like contagion, the kind of air that could sicken you. Tomorrow was another day and I did not know what would happen. Just like every other day.

I switched off the lights, stood there in darkness, enraptured by the shadows. I felt so lost that it took me a minute, maybe longer, to realize that the woman across the courtyard had started screaming again.

QUESTION NUMBER TWO:
WHAT TO DO?

My marriage was a shit show from the beginning. I say that with no self-pity, no play for sympathy. It's just the way it was, and that's all we have when everything is finished and done, regardless of the lies we tell. If I wasn't the catalyst, for a long time I was a willing participant. I can't say it any plainer than that.

And yet, my wife, she played a part as well. Not in the sense that everybody always plays a part in their own, or in their partner's, unraveling, but on the most specific terms. It was, after all, her idea. Not the end, but the other thing. The thing that led us into the uncanny valley of our dissolution, which was (how could it have been any different?) sex.

My wife was adventurous, let me say it plain. That was part of the attraction, from the moment I first saw her. She was one of those people, the ones that others notice, and I … I was a hanger-on. How we met is unimportant, but it was miraculous that she ever paid attention — or maybe blighted, given how it all worked out. That first night, we had been drinking; when we ended up at her place, it was as if I'd found myself. She was wild, she was naked, we stayed up until dawn together, and if this is all I am willing to say about it, that is not a matter of what I remember but rather of what I still desire to protect. I can see it all, everything that ever happened, all the stages, her at twenty and twenty-eight and thirty-three. I liked how she looked, I liked her ambition, I liked that she made money. I liked her tendency to take charge, to carry me in her wake. It was as if I didn't have to make decisions, as if all I had to do was go along. This was how we got married, how we wound up in California, and how we ended up, at long last and in an act that felt like nothing so much as an inevitability, with another man in our bed.

14

Another man in our bed. And what does it mean that it was her idea? Nothing, just a way to stave off boredom, although who was bored with whom? All of life, that's what it is, a way to stave off boredom, to hide, for a moment if we're lucky, from the inevitability of the closed box. Sometimes, I picture her that way, on her back, hands folded across her breasts, eyes closed, the pallor of her skin like wax lips, like pulled taffy, something not so much artificial as imagined, as if I have made her up. Certainly, that was true of the sex — from the beginning, she liked to push the boundaries: bondage, fantasy. One Saturday, she had me tie her to the bed and leave her there while I went about a list of chores she had left me, laundry, dishes, vacuuming the living room. By the time I joined her in bed, she was as worked up as I had ever seen her, although she did not wish to be untied. There … is that enough information? It makes me feel dirty even to share this, although it did not feel dirty, not at first, with her. Yes, dirty, like a betrayal, like I am telling secrets out of school. Sex was, for us, like a conspiracy, something we could take out when we were alone together and willing to be revealed. I am not a demure man, I am the opposite of chivalrous, and there was nothing demure about what we did with, and to, one another. I still want to keep those secrets, although I don't know her anymore.

Anyway, the other man in our bed. Not much to say about that except it had been a fantasy of hers from shortly after we arrived in Los Angeles. We were living in an apartment complex in North Hollywood, not so different from this one. Next door lived a couple who was into swinging, and one night my wife came home flushed. She had run into the husband; he had shown her pictures of his wife. I was too surprised to be angry, or perhaps I had supposed it all along. She was not suggesting we sleep with him, or them, although that door was clearly open; *Better*, she said, *not to shit where you eat.* After that, she grew increasingly insistent; she'd talk about it often, in and out of bed. It started with a few trips to high-end strip clubs, where she'd pay for a male dancer in a private room. The night we traversed that final boundary, we took a suite in a hotel. The other man was hired help; she didn't want any attachments, any complications, anything that might lead back to her. It started with cocktails, then dancing; she wanted me to watch. An hour or so later, as I sat at the end of the bed, my wife splayed out before me, eyes closed, lips twisted in a grimace of guilt and ecstasy, I knew we'd crossed our Rubicon.

Sunday, I woke up hung over. Sunlight peeked around the edges of my bedroom curtains like a stain. My eyes felt dry, as if they'd been drained of liquid. My head throbbed in bursts of beating blood.

I looked around the room, trying to remember. On the night table, a half empty glass of Maker's Mark. Never good when you bring your drink to bed with you, but I had no idea how I had gotten here. The last thing I recalled was cleaning the bathroom, taking out the trash.

Tell me Corrina, where you been so long?

And then that came back to me also, the sound of her screaming, and the conversation we'd had.

Conversation? Hardly. More like a set of notes. Like that glass of Maker's, a lead to follow. More and more, I found myself losing time or memory, waking up, as I just had, with no idea of what had happened the night before. Not a blackout, more a kind of dimness, what let's call an inner fog. It was the booze, of course it was, but not only — or should I say it was something more? Either way, I often found myself piecing things together in the morning, looking at my phone, my computer, to see if they offered any clues. It was a disconcerting feeling, going through your life this way. As if all we were was a set of traces, of detritus and clues. Sometimes, I would check my browser to find purchases, music mostly, stuff I'd come across on the internet, a harvest of unlikely fruits. Sometimes, what I found was darker, like the residue of a disembodied dream. It felt as if I were looking at a fingerprint left by my unconscious, the self I was when I was not around.

But it was also stuff I didn't want to look at, the expression of a me I didn't want to know. More than once, scrolling through my history, I was hit with a wave of revulsion so thick it felt as if I were drowning: not shame, for shame was redeemable, but something more encompassing, more perverse. Humiliation, maybe, or degradation, the way I had felt in that hotel room. To confront the evidence felt like looking into my own eyes in a mirror, and all they were casting back at me were blanks. I don't generally think about how I got here; in my marriage, in my life. It doesn't matter who we were or who we will be, only who we are. But these traces, they unsettled me, and not only because they came at a cost. No, they unsettled me because they suggested not a promise but its opposite, an indication, a set of symptoms, a reminder that there was something going on here, something more than the surfaces revealed.

I rubbed my eyes and tried to focus, felt their dryness sting. Nine thirty a.m. by the bedside clock. I didn't bother looking at my laptop; if I had been doing anything the night before, it was better left alone. Slowly, I pulled myself upright, first into a low slouch, then feet on the floor. My limbs were heavy, pummeled almost, as if I'd been beaten, as if I had run a thousand miles.

In the bathroom, more of it came drifting back, bits and pieces, how she'd looked and smelled. There was something about that streak of blue hair, I couldn't get it out of my head. Not that I wanted anything from her, or even anything to do with her, but we both lived here, across the courtyard, and there was the sense that things had been left unfinished, up in the air. Unfinished? More like: not even started, the whisper of something, its flashpoint, zygote of an idea. I used to know a kid in high school we called Zygote because his features appeared so undifferentiated; that was what this was. Yes, zygote — not even embryonic, and if I had anything to say about it, we would never get to that point. But already, I knew, I was past believing that this was just another fantasy.

As I was getting dressed, I heard the sound of

knocking; I didn't need to look. I let her wait while I combed my hair, still wet from the shower, threaded a belt through the loops of my pants. If I could take care of these small details, I was thinking, everything else might fall into place. She might wander off, or I might wake and discover that this was all a dream, that I had never come to California, that my wife was still around. The knocking didn't stop, however, and after another minute, I made my way to the front door. She was wearing shorts and a tank top, and when I opened it, she brushed past me as if I weren't even standing there.

As if this were not my place but hers.

"I don't know what happened," she said, once she was in the living room. There was no preamble; it was as if she were picking up where she'd left off. And why not? The residue of the night before still retained a spectral presence, as if the evening had never come to an end. On the table, the bottle — which I had remembered to cap, thankfully —and her glass. She didn't notice, or appear to notice; she was looking right at me. There was kohl, again, around her eyes, and bright red lipstick on her mouth. Her mouth that was moving, that was saying something, something I wasn't hearing …

"I'm sorry?"

She ran a hand through her hair. "I don't usually lose control like that …"

"What about the screaming?" I asked.

For a moment, she didn't answer, the air between us thick with heat. The smell of vomit had been replaced by the fresher scent of soap and shampoo, and a whisper of plumeria on the morning breeze. It felt like anything could happen, tragedy or transcendence… and then her mouth curled into a grin.

"Well, that," she laughed. "What I mean is: I don't usually lose control when I'm in someone else's home."

"Good to know," I said, but I was laughing also. "I'll keep that in mind."

"Anyway, I want to make it up to you. What are you doing for breakfast?"

Breakfast? I hadn't even thought about it. I was just glad to be standing upright. When I told her that, she nodded, as if something had been decided.

"Come on," she said. "I'm buying. Anything you like."

We ended up at the Farmer's Market, in a booth at Dupar's. She drove us in the Prius she kept parked out on the street. The Sunday crowd was thick but not so much that we had to wait. It had been a long time since I'd been here; I'd forgotten about this place. We sat across from one another, ordered eggs and coffee, and I felt the caffeine cut the fog in my brain like a dull knife. No artisanal blends here, just a dishwater diner brew as bland as the look I tried to plaster across my face. I was thinking about last night, trying to reconstruct the missing pieces, and my plan was to let her do the talking until I figured out more fully where I stood.

"I love this place, it never changes," she said after we'd been served. "I used to come here with my dad."

I looked at her, my eyes empty, waiting to see where this would lead.

"He liked places like this: diners, burger stands. We used to go to Tommy's, Cassell's ... the real Los Angeles, he called it, the one the tourists never see."

I tried to picture her, a young girl, holding the hand of an older man, but the image blurred into indistinction. I couldn't imagine his face, his body; he was just a cloud to me, grayed out of the picture, translucent as a ghost.

"After my mother died ..." her voice evaporated in a whisper trail ... "when he was trying to be a parent. He had no skill for it. We never really knew each other. But we were all we had. Part of what we'd do was go out, eat fries and burgers, pretend nothing had changed. Pretend she'd be waiting for us when we got home, and the burden would be lifted. The burden of us figuring out how to get along."

"I'm sorry," I croaked, voice raspy from disuse.

"It was a long time ago," she said, eyes focusing on something in the middle distance, over my shoulder.

"Anyway," she went on, "after a while, all that faded. We stopped trying, and then my dad ... well, he got married again."

"To your stepmother."

"Yes." She laughed, mouth a red slash. "Evil fucking witch."

I waited for her to continue, but that was that, it seemed. I forked some eggs into my mouth, drank more coffee, counting out the seconds — five, ten, twenty, sixty — as the silence ballooned between us like a presence in its own right.

"How did he die?" I asked, finally, when it seemed that she would never speak again. Even as I did, I wondered if this was the whole point, the intention, if she had been working me.

"My father?" she said. "He had a heart attack. Three months ago. Sixty-five years old. Never sick a day in his life — isn't that how the cliché goes? Until he dropped fucking dead."

Something was picking at me, some piece of information, some distant memory or clue. She seemed wistful today, mournful about her father — except I wasn't sure this was correct. *We weren't close ... I didn't like him.* Isn't that what she had said last night? And it was in that booth, plate of eggs before me, that I became aware, for the first time, of that sense of water folding in above me, as if I had been submerged. I thought of Shakespeare: *There are more things in heaven and earth ... than are dreamt of in your philosophy.* Hinting at so much and yet at nothing, at the inability of the universe to be contained. That's how I felt sitting there. *More things in heaven and earth ...* and here I was, just one of them, and she another, and her intent unfathomable to me. I had the idea that she was building to something, that some agenda had been put in play here, that I was being pulled in against my will. And yet, will — what was it? Did I know? It had required so much just to come here, to sit across the table from her. She was talking again, I could hear her, but I couldn't figure out what any of it meant. Did she love him? Did she hate him? Were those the right or necessary questions? Could it be that it was more complicated, that the answer was both?

I didn't have to wait long, as it happened, to find out.

She smiled as if she knew what I was thinking. Then, in a weirdly formal gesture, she reached out a hand, which she put on top of mine. I startled; it had been a long time since I'd been touched by anybody other than myself. She laughed, patted my hand, said, "Don't worry, it's not like that."

I must have looked even more perplexed because she withdrew her hand, before continuing: "I was hoping you might do a favor for me."

Again, I waited, letting her take the lead. I was having trouble thinking, trouble making sense of where we were. Her lips were moving; I tried to zero in on them, to read the shape of the words that she was speaking, to break the code. A few phrases began to assert themselves: *hire you; check in on my stepmother; see what her intentions are.*

"Wait, what?" I asked. "What are you saying?"

I needed to slow everything down.

"I want to hire you," she repeated, stretching out the words, enunciating every syllable, as if she were talking to a child or an idiot, "to check in on my stepmother and see if you can find out what her intentions are."

I tried to tell her that this wasn't what I did, that it wasn't what I had ever done, that it had nothing to do with who I was. I wasn't sure if the words were making sense. As I talked, her face folded into an ironic grin.

"You must need the money," she said. "You don't seem to have a job."

"No, I guess. Not really." I didn't like that she'd been watching me.

"I'll pay you two hundred dollars to go and talk to her."

"To talk?" Again, it was as if her words refused

to register, as if she were speaking a language I had never learned.

"Just talk. I need to know. My father gave me an allowance. Monthly. For the moment, the estate is still paying out. But she's trying to make that go away. Has her lawyers working on it. It's all part of cutting me out of the inheritance." She paused, took a sip of coffee, set the cup down with a gesture so measured, so precise that it was touching, as if her whole life depended on placing it just right. "After they got married, I stopped coming around. Not that I was there much anyway. She made it … difficult. Always demanding his attention. Like she was trying to push us apart."

"Where does she live?" I asked, looking for some traction. I wasn't sure I wanted to get involved.

"Benedict Canyon," she said. "The house where I grew up." She paused. "She's trying to take everything from me. If she wins, I'll have nothing left."

And I should have gotten up right then, the moment she brought up winning, the moment she framed it in such terms. It was a competition — or worse, a battle — and to become a part of it would mean having to take sides. But two hundred dollars? Just for talking? She was right, I hadn't worked in quite some time. I had a bit of money, a little nest egg, you might call it. It wasn't much but it had been enough that I could spend my days staying out of trouble. It had been enough that I'd be left alone. Now, however, it was dwindling, and it wasn't like I had anything else going on.

"Okay," I said, "I can go up there tomorrow. What's her number?"

"No, no," she hissed, leaning across the table until her face was tight and close to mine. Her features blurred into a mash of flesh tones; I couldn't keep them distinct. "Don't tip it off, don't let her know you're coming. She plays tennis in the mornings; she'll be coming off the court around noon, and you can catch her unprepared."

Coming off the court … coming off the court. Back in my apartment after Corrina dropped me off, I kept hearing that phrase echo through my head. It was like the chorus in a blues song, redolent of so much at once. The tennis court, of course, and also the courtroom where, I had to assume, this family drama was heading, if it hadn't been there yet. But more than that, the layers of the conflict, money and love and loss and privilege, not unlike Los Angeles itself.

People say Los Angeles is superficial, but that's not true. Sure, it's got its flash and sizzle, low-slung cars and hilltop mansions, billboards and Botox and the sad, sad hustle of celebrity, all those people trying to be famous, trying to be seen. But this is just a facet, or an overlay. The real city unfolds in apartment complexes and bungalow courts, in the sprawl of neighborhoods over crests and flatlands, in four million people trying to make it through the day. Even the wealthy … they still eat and shit and breathe and long for something: love or lust or soul connection, some meaning to the dull parade of hours. I was like that too, alone in a life I couldn't say that I had chosen, although I couldn't say, either, that I had not. And Corrina, poor little rich girl, still looking for her daddy's affection, even though he was dead and it was a done deal, even though her heart was full of ghosts. *Coming off the court* — it was as if a game had ended but not really, as if we were all caught in the aftermath. Or no, not aftermath but transition, in a moment that had no definition, that was neither here nor there.

When I was younger, I became interested in a being called a tulpa, which is an emanation of the mind. Tulpas don't exist, in other words, not really — although, I guess the point is, who's to say? I can't remember where I heard about them, but the idea was that a Buddhist monk or holy man would dream a tulpa into being so he could have physical relief, or satisfaction, without betraying his vows. I was intrigued by this — release without guilt, without attachment — and it made me wonder: How real could imagination get? Did it matter if something, anything, were there, had happened, if we believed it to be so? The answer, of course, is no; just look around. Los Angeles may be an actual city, filled with actual people, but some of those people ... well, let's just say there's an unbridgeable gap between what they think is happening and the situation on the ground. In any event, these tulpas. As it turns out, they are not so easy to control. If you imagine them fully enough, so much that you start to see and feel them, they take on a spirit, an autonomy, of their own. I only learned this part later, after I read up on the subject; they were not, I came to understand, about intimacy at all. This must have been after I was married, when my wife and I had both begun to look for something, some spark, some lost connection that, we were discovering, might not have ever been there. Tulpas again, as if we were tulpas for one another, as if we had dreamed each other into being. And then, once we were embodied, we had each gone our own way. What do we know, after all, of other people, even (or especially) those closest to us, those with whom we share our lives? I'd had such thoughts before, but today, in the flat hot stillness after returning from breakfast, I could not get these questions out of my mind.

The apartment was stifling, but I didn't raise the windows; I liked the feeling of being enclosed. Or not liked, but wanted, needed, a way to keep my distance from the world. Why had I said yes, why was I getting into this? It wasn't as if the two hundred dollars was going to make a difference in my life. I needed to make a change, a real change, and this was just a detour, a bit of voyeurism, really, curiosity or prurience pushed out into three dimensions, a way to pass a little time. What would I do tomorrow otherwise? Just sit here in the living room and sweat. For a moment, I was struck with a sense of longing so sharp it was like a knife had cut me open, but then it faded, as it generally does, to a dull ache beneath the skin.

Across the courtyard, Corrina's place lay dark and shuttered; after breakfast, she had gone away. Errands, maybe, or a social engagement; she did not tell me and I didn't ask. Like my wife ... who knew where she was, what she was doing? Wherever the dead go, whatever they do. She is dead to me, after all, dead in my imagination, like something I invented and then threw away. We are all projections, tulpas in our own minds, nothing is real on any lasting terms. Even the continents, they drift and move upon a sea of molten magma, crashing and reconstituting, matter begetting matter, entropy and energy. How can the world be an actual place when we can disappear from it, when our whole lives we are disappearing, pulling away from one another, moving apart? Some days, it is all I can do to see anything as solid, as more than heat lines wavering off the pavement, blurring what is right in front of me into mirage.

I went into the bedroom, looked through the closet, wondering what I ought to wear. I wanted to make an impression, although what kind I didn't know. I had a suit — blue, off the rack — and a white shirt and red tie. They hung there with a few other button-downs, and on the floor, a loose heap of shoes and sneakers, and a shovel in a plastic bag. I'd bought the shovel not long after moving in; I'd had the notion to landscape the dry patch of bushes adjacent to my front door. I had never done anything about it, though, and now, the shovel lay unused in the back of my closet like the expression of some stillborn hope. It made me sad each time my eyes fell across it. But still, I couldn't give it up.

There was an advantage in wearing the suit, I thought: to look official, on my game. But there was also an advantage in going the other way, in showing up as myself, khakis and a tee shirt, keeping expectations low. What had I been thinking, saying I'd go up there? I knew nothing about any of this. Nothing about her stepmother, nothing about their money, nothing about Corrina except that last night or this morning, she had made a decision, that she liked me or could use me, or maybe it was both.

As for me, I was having trouble remembering anything about her, what she looked like, the sound of her voice.

I opened my computer, thinking I might do a

Google search for Corrina's father, see if I could find anything of use. Then I realized that I didn't even know his name. I had no choice but to go up there without any information. Although maybe it was better just to take the plunge.

I decided I would wear the suit and tie. The veneer of authority, that was what I needed. I didn't need anything more. Everything else could come later, if there was a later. In the meantime, there was nothing else to know.

Before I got up from the laptop, I made sure to clear my history, taking care to avert my eyes.

Avert my eyes, avert my eyes — the key to sanity, especially now that I was being drawn into something I did not understand.

"I can't think about that right now," I said aloud to the empty room. "If I do, I'll go crazy. I'll think about that tomorrow."

Whatever was waiting for me out there, I would deal with it when it arrived.

QUESTION NUMBER THREE:
WILL YOU DINE AND DANCE WITH ME?

Corrina's stepmother was beautiful. I wasn't expecting that. I stood on the front steps of her house in the hills wearing my blue suit and my red tie. I was neat, clean, shaved, and sober, and I didn't care who knew it.

House? Estate was more like it, set into a tumbling slope of landscaped grounds. Corrina had conveniently left this part out, although perhaps she didn't see it that way. It's hard to know what people recognize, what they take for granted. It could have been that this was just home, just what she was used to ... except she was in a dispute over money, living on an allowance that was generous enough that, like me, she didn't appear to have to work. And generous enough, too, that it was something to fight over, which made me think she knew what it was worth.

It was noon, and the sun was a sledgehammer, beating down on me from the center of the sky. I stood there sweating in my suit and tie, feeling the shirt stick to my back. The heat was like a woolen blanket; it was hard to take more than a shallow breath. I had looked for a tennis court when I'd arrived, listened for the thwack of ball and racquet, the soft pock of footfall on clay or composite. Maybe I was late, or maybe it was too hot, but no one was on the grounds. There was a circular driveway with a fountain that was running water, which told me something about Corrina's stepmother, her priorities. I rang the doorbell and I waited, listening to the sound of it — a resonant clatter, like church bells — echo behind the massive oak front door.

When the door finally swung open, it took a moment to adjust. All I could see was blackness, like a negative image, canceling out the world. As my vision settled, I could make out the shape of a woman. Short skirt, sleeveless top and a smell that was both sweet and bitter, like a cross between sandalwood and sweat. If she'd been playing tennis, it was before I got here. She had showered and dressed. I wavered in the sunlight, wondering if I were being set up, waiting for what would happen next.

"Can I help you?" she asked, and her voice cut like the sound of falling blades. My vision cleared a little further and I could make out her eyes now, gray as steel, staring back at me.

"Hello," I said, and mumbled my name, adding that I didn't mean to intrude. We both knew this was a lie. She stood in the doorway, right hip jutting as if to block me, elbow bent and cocked. I was pretending, that much was obvious, but neither of us could quite say what it meant. "Your stepdaughter asked if I'd come by and see you," I continued finally, and then, after she didn't say anything: "Corrina?"

"I know who my stepdaughter is." She gave me a quick once-over, hair to shoes. "Are you a private investigator? Because I know you're not a cop."

"Just a friend," I said, wondering why I had come here, how I was going to extricate myself.

"How much is she paying you?"

I looked at her again, and then away. "Two hundred."

"Jesus," she muttered quickly, as if the word scalded her mouth, and had to be cooled with spit. "I guess you get what you pay for." She stepped aside, clearing a passage through the doorway. "You may as well come in."

The foyer was open, arching, two storeys tall, like an English country manor. As I entered, I really got a look at her, curve of calf, swell of breast, hair thick and brushed out, cut just below the shoulder, gray shot through with streaks of brown. She had to be fifty-five, maybe older, and she was the most striking woman I had ever seen. Not because she had preserved herself but rather because she hadn't: no Botox, no plastic surgery, no trims or tucks or realignments, just the natural prime of middle age. She carried herself with the assurance of entitlement; I could see that from the first. She didn't wait, just shut the door and walked away. Follow? Don't follow? It was up to me. One minute into our encounter and she had already seized the power; I was playing catch-up in a game whose rules remained a mystery.

And I couldn't take my eyes off her, so what else was I going to do? I crept across the black and white tile floor, moving from one square to the next like a piece in a game of chess. She was clearly the queen, moving as she saw fit; I wanted to think of myself as a knight, or even a bishop, but I was just a pawn. One step at a time, one square at a time. As I finished crossing the entryway, I saw her, through an open rectory door, standing in a small room, walls paneled in light oak, furniture heavy, leather-bound, like the accoutrements of a club. Her back was to me, and when she turned, I could see that she had been fixing herself a drink.

"Can I offer you something?" she asked. Her face was a set of smooth planes, giving nothing away.

"Whatever you're having is fine."

"One club soda coming up," she said, and there must have been something in my face, in the wilt of my shoulders, because she stopped and looked at me, actually looked at me, for the first time. I could see her measuring, taking inventory, as if a lens were being tightened and turned. "Unless you'd like something stronger...?" she added, eyes glinting with revelation. She looked satisfied, like she had figured out a key piece of information, something I didn't want her to know.

"I suppose you could twist my arm."

"Suit yourself," she said, as if something had been settled. And perhaps something had. I had come here thinking I might make the usual inquiries. I had come here as if I were a character in a novel or a film. Get her talking and see what she would tell me. See if she would make a slip. I had come here looking to put one over. I had come here looking for an easy win. But by the time we sat down, facing each other in two of those club chairs, I knew I had already lost.

29

Her name was Sylvia. Sylvia Glenn. She told me that as she sat before me, crossing and uncrossing her legs. Mostly I just watched, wanting to leave and wanting never to leave.

"So how do you know Corrina?" she asked, and when I said we were neighbors in the apartment complex, she nodded, as if something else had been confirmed. Every word I said was like a piece in a puzzle she was building in her head. "So what you're saying," she went on, "is that you don't know her, not really? That yours is a connection of circumstance?"

Connection of circumstance. I found myself drawn to the formality of her phrasing, in that wood and leather room. The sensation was like going downhill, fast, in a car with no breaks, the buzzing in my stomach like a hive of bees. I nodded, not sure what I was admitting, or if I was admitting anything at all. I was here by my own choice. No one had coerced me. But she seemed to be suggesting something different, suggesting it without actually suggesting it, or perhaps it was just that I had never been much good at reading the signs.

"She told you about the inheritance?" she asked. I started to respond but she held up a hand. "I would expect as much ..." she murmured, and now she was ticking off points as if they were items on a list. "So that means she also told you about me and her father, and the dispute over the will? It's all true, of course. I don't want her to get a dime." She paused, her face an open question, as if waiting for me to make Corrina's case. "I can only guess what she has told you, but that girl has never done anything except take money from her father. Even now that he is dead and buried. She only cares about herself. I'll bet she told you how close they were, didn't she?" I said nothing but my face must have been a giveaway. "She always says that," she continued, "except when she is saying the opposite. Look" — and now she leaned forward, peering out at me through slitted eyelids as if she were sharing some sort of secret — "I've known that girl a long time, since before her mother died, and she has never wanted for anything.

That's her problem, everything was always handed to her, she never had to earn it. It's made her spoiled."

"I don't know anything about that. I just met her." But I was remembering the screaming, once a week or so for the last few months, the tantrums of an overgrown child. I thought about her boots, stylish, expensive, and what she was paying me. But then, I wasn't doing anything either, or I wouldn't have taken on this job.

"I know she thinks of me as her wicked stepmother, and to some extent, she's right. Hell, I even live in a castle ..." and here, she broke into a low laugh. The sound was rich and throaty, but also a little sad. It left me with the impression of her alone at the top of her hill, insulated from the city below. I imagined her at night, standing on the front lawn, unable even to see the lights below. It was like a vacuum up here, deep space, another place to remove oneself from the world.

"But here's the thing," Sylvia added, her eyes sharpening, her voice growing pointed and tight. "I have no intention of backing off. You can call that selfish, and it might be — I lived with him, not her. But I also have to tell you: She's a monster in the making. She's had a free ride her whole life. Thinks the world exists at her whim, at her pleasure. Just look at you, running up here like her errand boy."

"I'm not her errand boy," I said, but my voice was sullen, like a child who had been thwarted.

"Sure you're not," she said. "Two hundred dollars." She gave me the once-over again, mouth curling into a slick smile. "That's some bargaining you did there. I hope it was worth your while. Now, why don't you go back down the hill and tell my *step*daughter that she can fuck herself?"

She settled in her chair and took a sip of her club soda, the picture of privileged charm. The conversation was over, there was nothing else to say. I drank also, felt the heat radiate across my tongue. Another pull and the warmth expanded, tickling the edges of my brain.

"If you'll excuse me," she said. "Unless there was

something else?"

I stood, hand still wrapped around the empty glass, unsure where to put it now that I was done. Her face was impassive, as if etched in stone. For a moment, I took it in. Those cheekbones, high, their color. Lips thin but also full, no lipstick, like an impression or a sketch. Her presence provoked an unexpected feeling. I didn't want to know. She had just dismissed me — and why not? I was wasting her time — but I lingered anyway. I lowered my eyes, took in the subtle sculpture of her ankle, tendons like pulse points. What had I been thinking? I was completely overmatched.

Just as I was about to put the glass down, she unfolded from her chair. It was like watching a dance, or a flower open, unconnected to anything but itself. If we could just stay here, if this moment didn't have to lead to another ... it was as lithe and lovely as anything I had seen. And yet, at the same time, self-contained, or self-directed, no wasted movement of any kind. It was the gesture of someone who knew what she was doing, what she wanted, who was not lost, had never been. It was the gesture of someone who would not give up, not ever, and all of a sudden, I understood that she had not been born rich, that this was not her natural habitat. She had not possessed or enjoyed privilege early, but instead had fought to get here. It was something she had worked for. It was marriage as a job.

"Let me take that," she said, and she reached for the glass, her fingers closing, for the briefest instant, over mine. They were cool, as if not fully blooded, and they rested for just a little longer than they had to: a message, not an oversight. Our eyes met, and locked; I counted one and two before I looked away. The glass slipped from my hand, but hers was there to catch it. Or no — not catch it, because she had never let it go.

"A piece of advice, if I may." Her voice was soft and insinuating, her face less than a foot from mine. "Be careful around my stepdaughter. She can be dangerous. Although perhaps you already know that. She and I, well ..."

Her voice faded and she turned away.

"Never mind. Enough said. I assume you can find your own way out."

I knocked on Corrina's door but she was not at home. Who knew where she was in the middle of a Monday? I did not have her cell and she did not have mine; she had thought it would be better that way. *Why?* I had asked, but she'd insisted: *No digital paper trail,* she said. I couldn't see why it would matter, unless her stepmother was right and she really was dangerous, which meant there was something going on here that I couldn't see.

I went home and poured a drink, tried to piece together what I knew. But the stepmother, Sylvia — her face kept pushing other thoughts aside. There was something about her, something scary, or at least intimidating, and yet I was drawn to her, as well. She was like a wild animal, beautiful to look at, but you knew you had to be careful, that she could turn on you at any time.

Be careful. It was what she'd said about Corrina, the warning she had given me. What did it mean? What was I missing? Corrina was adrift, that much was true, something of a lost soul. But I was lost myself, or in between ... between the cracks of a life, of a universe, that had stopped paying attention, if indeed it ever had. She seemed soft, yes — spoiled even, to use her stepmother's word — but couldn't that be a function of the way she looked? Those angular features floating on the round field of her face. It was as if her edge, her sharpness, was conditional, as if she changed depending on the angle or the light. Caught from the proper perspective, she was captivating, or she could be, although that effect had only fleetingly taken hold of me. Her stepmother, though; she was captivating without trying.

Or perhaps it was the not trying that was the key.

In any case, the visit. What had I been doing there? I'd arrived like something in a Raymond Chandler novel, calling on however many million dollars. But I didn't know anything of that world. I didn't even know what questions to ask, let alone how to ask them, which was probably why she'd invited me in. A game, just a game she and Corrina were playing, high stakes chess and me a piece moved first by one and then the other, until I didn't know which way to turn. The more I thought about it, the more I started to get angry, to wonder if I had been used. But how, why? I couldn't work it out. Corrina had to have known what would happen. And yet, she had paid me to go up there anyway.

I finished the drink and fixed another, watched the hands of the clock go around on the wall. I sat in the living room, eyes fixed on Corrina's door across the courtyard. I wouldn't have called it a vigil exactly, although it was true that I was waiting for her to come back. I took off my jacket and hung it up, loosened my tie and rolled my sleeves. I couldn't say why, but I wanted to be wearing these clothes when I saw her, if only so she could see I'd taken the assignment seriously.

It was after five when I heard the click of boot heels on the concrete of the courtyard path and watched Corrina cross to her front door. On her step sat a small hibachi, dusty from disuse. She was wearing skinny jeans and a sleeveless top, like a million women in Hollywood. Alone, she looked more focused, more determined, as if with no one watching, she could unveil a truer self. Still, what was that truer self? Did it exist? Or were we all, always, playacting our way through life? Look at me, sitting for hours in my apartment in a tie and shirtsleeves, as if the outfit gave me something I could use. Who was I really? How much was make-believe? I might imagine the Corrina I was seeing through the window was the real one, but who knew how she felt? Even walking alone to her front door was — it had to be — a performance, a construction, the expression of a public face. Was she different when she was alone inside her apartment? She had to be, with all the screaming, although I didn't expect that I'd find out.

The same questions applied to me, as well. What

was I doing here but waiting, for an outcome I could not anticipate? Whenever I thought of the future, a world beyond this moment, all I could imagine was a blank. Whenever I tried to project out, to think about where I might be going, I couldn't see the road. Progress was another myth, another illusion; the only possible outcome was entropy. *Lack of order or predictability*, gradual decline into disorder. And didn't that describe *everything?* I thought about the streets outside, Franklin Avenue with its patches and its potholes, the slow degrading collapse of the hills. Sometimes, after a heavy rain, an entire outcropping would dissolve, tumble down on boulevards and houses, as if the world were made of sand. I thought about the man I often saw in the neighborhood, walking in a brown UCLA sweatshirt, white hair a greasy tangle rising off his head. He was always muttering, scowling, as if even to be here was its own sort of affront. Occasionally, he appeared to notice me, or at least he would react as if he did. A shake of his head, a small string of invective, as if I had disappointed him, or let him down. Once, I'd heard him say: "My instrument." Once, I'd heard him say: "You lied to me." I couldn't tell if he was talking to me or to himself.

Maybe it was that he seemed to see me. Maybe it was that he recognized me for who I was. I thought about those cars, torched by a disrupter, an agent of chaos whose chaos had gone silent. Silence ... that was what awaited. The only outcome that deserved the name.

I felt a flutter in my chest, a rising bubble of anxiety, felt it harden into a solid shape. Something in my throat, blocking my breathing, something that I couldn't swallow down. I poured another drink, put on some music; I needed to get out of my head. The system clicked and hummed, like an air conditioner switching on. Then, Merle Haggard, "Sing Me Back Home," those finger-picked arpeggios, and the chorus with its harmonies. The sound was thin, sweet and sour and sweet again. It oozed across the afternoon like honey, as if the Pied Piper had come to town. Haggard had done a version of "Corrine, Corrina," in the style of Wills. As I thought about that, I saw

35

Corrina's door open, watched her upper body reappear. There was something different about her, something that was not quite at ease. She craned her neck and I could see her nostrils quiver, as if she were sniffing smoke. Slowly, the rest of her emerged, like a stick figure unfolding, an outline not quite in three dimensions, slipping along the porous boundaries of the world.

I sat quiet when I heard her knocking. I didn't want her to think that I'd been waiting, after all. I finished my drink, and poured another, then went to the door as if I were some white-collar worker at the end of a long day. I could see myself, as if I were watching a reel of film unspool. Tie, shirtsleeves, tumbler, a real adult almost, some throwback archetype. She giggled when she saw me, her eyes a little pinned. I moved in closer; beneath the floral perfume, same as the other night, I could pick up the skunky trace of cannabis.

"That's what you wore up there?" she laughed. "She must have loved that."

"Saw right through me. In a second. That's the only reason she let me in."

My voice was low, with the slightest oscillating quaver. I hadn't realized I was angry until I began to speak. "Why did you ask me to go up there? There was no point to it. You had to have known that." I looked at her, directly into those dilated pupils. "What game are we playing here?"

I don't know what I was expecting: nothing probably. I don't know how I felt. But I wasn't ready for what happened. All of a sudden, her gaze sharpened, and her lips tightened into a thin red line. "Let's not discuss this outside, shall we?" she said. "May I come in?" Without waiting for a response, she elbowed past me, entering my living room, once more, as if it belonged to her.

Dangerous, I thought. *Be careful.* I had seen this side of her. The entitled side, don't take no for an answer, living out her exile in Hollywood until the money train pulled in. What did I know about her? Nothing. What did I know about her history? Just that I'd listened to her across the courtyard, listened as she screamed all those nights. Once again, I felt my anxiety rising.

What if Sylvia were right?

Yet once the door had shut behind us, her shoulders slumped and her eyes lost focus, and she sprawled into my chair and gestured at the Maker's. I went to the kitchen and got her a glass. There was no danger, this was just the woman who'd thrown up in my bathroom, a little reckless, a little out of control. She was an amateur, she didn't know what she was doing, she had thought I might intimidate her stepmother, which only proved how inexperienced we both were. Neither of us spoke as she sipped the liquor. Then she looked up, as if remembering where she was, that we were in each other's presence, and she asked, "She let you in?"

"Yes. Wasn't that the whole idea?"

"I guess so." She seemed confused, unsteady. "But I'm still surprised."

"If you didn't think she would let me in, why did you send me?"

"I was hoping you might catch her off her guard."

"Off her guard?"

"She always seems so sure of everything, like she's got all the answers. I wanted to knock her off her game."

"I hardly knocked her off her game," I said. "I didn't even catch her coming off the court. She was all clean and dressed when I arrived. She laughed when I told her why I'd come."

"Yeah, but you intrigued her. You must have, or she would have shut you out."

"Either that, or she thought I was so insignificant it didn't matter."

"It *doesn't* matter," she said. "The only thing that matters is you got in."

I was going to ask her why when I saw that she had gone off again. She was flexing her boots against the edge of my coffee table, looking into her glass, its amber liquid, as if it were a reliquary. What was she seeing there?

Not the future. And, I had to believe, not the past. Just the present, just this moment, on the couch in a stranger's apartment, in a territory neither one of us could comprehend. I watched her feet as she sat there. It was as if I couldn't help myself. I loved those boots, the shape of them. They recalled to me the press of a heel against my skin.

And yet, the more I sat with her, the more I became aware of other feelings, more inchoate. It was as if this were a performance, a gesture on the surface of the skin. The whole thing made me feel bad, made me want to go away.

"Excuse me," I said. "I just …" My voice faded as I went into the bathroom, where I put the toilet cover down and sat for a long count of one hundred, until my breathing grew regulated again.

When I came out, she was sitting upright, her feet flat on the floor. Her eyes were still, giving away nothing, Her face was composed.

"Can I ask you something?" I said. She nodded. "I still want to know: why did you ask me to go there?"

I thought she wasn't going to answer, either that or that she would shine me on. Her shoulders tightened but then eased, as if she'd let her disapproval pass.

"I'm not sure," she said. "I wanted to … I don't know, I wanted her to know that I am out here, that I am standing in her way."

"But are you?" I asked. "Do you have a lawyer? That's the only way you'll get her to back down."

"I hate lawyers," she said. "But yes, I have one. It's so much money. I guess I thought if we could just sit down together …"

"So you want me to represent your interests in that way."

"Represent my interests? That suit is getting to you." She laughed. "But yes — that's exactly what I want. To see how she'd react to you when you went up there. If she turned you away, that would be one thing. But she actually let you in."

"So you were using me."

"No, not using. Just testing the waters."

"From where I sit, it's the same thing."

"I'm sorry," she said. "I just …"

She paused, finished her drink, reached out to pour another. She never asked or looked at me to see if I had anything to say. I gave her the up and down as her stepmother had done to me. The situation was reversed. Here she was, in *my* living room, drinking *my* booze, while I waited for her to get to the point. I was starting to see what she was doing, starting to see beneath the surface, as it were. I wanted her to leave here, go back to her own apartment. I wanted not to see her, not to talk to her, again. This had as much to do with me as it did with her. I wanted to retreat. There was a reason I lived alone, a reason I knew no one, a reason every job or relationship I'd ever had ended up in flames. I liked to make believe it had to do with seeing through the bullshit, but the truth was that it had to do with me.

She took another sip of whiskey, nodding as if something had been decided. Then she turned her pinned eyes toward me.

"What I mean is, would you go see her again? I'll pay you another two hundred dollars."

"Make it five," I said, "and you've got yourself a deal."

QUESTION NUMBER FOUR: OUT THE DOOR?

I wasn't in it for the money. It wasn't that much money, after all. I was interested — in Sylvia, yes, but also in seeing how far this might go. I didn't know people like this and they intrigued me. And if I could make a little cash in the meantime, so much the better. But mainly, after what had begun to feel like a lifetime sentence in the cell of this apartment, I was getting a taste of the other side.

And yet, the other side ... the other side ... the other side of what? The other side of this life. I'd been in my head for so long, bound and gagged by the limits of everything I thought I'd come to understand. One more construction, one more performance. Even when I was alone. Now I wanted out. Not that I believed this would change anything. But it might offer a new costume, a new role.

As for the five hundred dollars, it didn't hurt. My rent was paid. But there was no long-term strategy. And yet, what was a long-term strategy, anyway? The only long-term strategy worthy of the name was the one that ended in the grave.

No, it was something else, a way of treading water, a way of biding time. A way of seeing what I could get away with, I suppose. I had the vague idea of trying to play them against each other, of seeing if Sylvia and I might become allied. Partly, this was physical; I couldn't get the image of her out of my mind. Her flint-gray eyes and those ankles, like an infrastructure of their own. I liked that she was smart, tough-minded, I liked that she was inaccessible in her way.

She scared me a little, and I liked that, as well.

Corrina, on the other hand, Corrina did not scare me. Corrina was a child playing with toys. After she'd agreed to give me the five hundred — no argument, I

40

should have asked for twice as much — she spent another hour in my living room, drinking my booze. It was like she had a sense of ... I don't know, let's call it ownership, as if because she had paid me, she had a right to anything she might want. At one point, she went into the kitchen, began to rummage through the refrigerator, permission neither asked nor granted, as if this were her home. *What are you doing?* I wanted to ask, but the heat, the lassitude — I couldn't be bothered, or perhaps I didn't care. After she came back, with a plate of crackers, she peered around the room with probing eyes. She picked up a stack of mail I'd left on the coffee table: bills and advertising circulars, nothing special. But nevertheless mine.

"Excuse me?" I said, pointing at the envelopes.

"Sorry. Bad habit. I used to do it to my father all the time."

"I'm not your father," I responded, smiling to soften the moment. She nodded, laughed, and put the letters down, but there was a coldness — or more accurately, a blankness — behind her eyes.

"No," she said at last. "But you're going to help me with my father."

And again, I felt the breathy whisper of conspiracy. Her father? Was he at the center of this? I thought it had been about the money. But then, if I wasn't in it for the money, how could I expect that she would be?

I wanted to know more, to understand the dynamics. But I wasn't an investigator. Sylvia had seen through that right away. I was just a guy with no real skills, in a small apartment in Hollywood, on the hook for what, I didn't know. I did have a computer, though, and now I knew Corrina's family name. After she left, I did what I should have done the moment I encountered her: Do a search, see what information that might yield.

There wasn't much: social media, mostly. Privacy settings at their highest, which meant I couldn't see a lot. A few scattered photos: one, perhaps a decade old, showing Corrina in a sorority sweater, with a bunch of other young women, on a campus that looked as if it were in Southern California, although I couldn't tell exactly which one. No listings, no quotations, no donations, not many friends or followers; with few exceptions, it was as if her whole life was a puff of smoke.

Her father, however, that gave me something, maybe something I could use. He'd had an obituary in the *Times*, not a big one, but a few paragraphs. Everything was as she'd said: dead of a heart attack at sixty-five. He'd been a doctor, sports medicine, until he invented an artificial tendon, a bit of high-performance rubber that flexed like a piston or a strut. He had sold the patent, after which he'd never practiced medicine again, although that's not to say that he retired, not exactly; the obituary said he'd gone on to dabble in real estate. The inheritance Corrina and Sylvia were contesting was in the vicinity of thirty million dollars. Everyone could have a piece and still be satisfied. The article was accompanied by a photo from a charity event: he was gray-haired, nondescript, wearing a tuxedo, flanked by Magic Johnson and Tommy Lasorda. Through the computer screen, his features didn't quite cohere.

Sylvia, it turned out, had been a nurse; that was how they'd met. For a moment, I wondered if he had been struck by her at first sight, by the delicate turn of those ankles, the electric buzzing of those eyes. I imagined them working in close proximity in a hospital or office, imagined him coming home to a wife he no longer loved and a distant daughter, imagined all his longing and his loss. Had they been together before his first wife died? How had she died, for that matter? The obituary offered no information on that. All it said was that he'd married Sylvia two years later, and that she'd been with him when he fell. I clicked on the photo to make it larger; the details pixelated out of sight. So close, almost as if I could reach through the screen and touch him. This might be how his widow and his daughter also felt.

Thirty million dollars and here I was asking

for chump change. Two hundred here, five hundred there. Story of my life, inability to see the big picture, to recognize what was right in front of me. And yet, the more I thought about it, the more a question began to pick at me: with all that money, why was Corrina living here? She had an allowance from the estate, that much I knew, but she hadn't moved in recently. And whatever was happening now with the money, when her father had been alive, she could have (couldn't she?) asked for anything.

I wondered how long she had been here. I wondered how she'd managed to stay. All that screaming … hadn't anyone complained about it? The property manager didn't seem the type to let it slide. I'd met him when I signed the lease, a blank slate of a guy named John, who wore matching shorts and tee shirts, a baseball cap. He was a graduate of some hospitality program that had taught him everything except hospitality. I almost never saw him, but on the rare occasions he came to the complex, he was almost always picking at someone: the gardeners for how they did or didn't landscape, some tenant late on the rent. Still, there she was, across the courtyard, carrying on to her heart's content. I wondered how much she — or the estate — was paying for the privilege. Maybe that was part of the deal.

I did a search for the lawsuit, but it had not yet been brought to court. There were no affidavits, no details, no information for me to peruse. Limits of technology: it only answers the questions you already know to ask. No, I was going to need to do some digging — a process, I realized, that Sylvia could help me with.

I asked the Lyft driver to leave me around the corner, on foot in a neighborhood of Porsches and Teslas, which marked me as out of place. I was wearing the suit and tie again, and it was hot: even on the brief walk, up a short slope to the circle of her driveway, perspiration began to bead along my back and sides. At the door, I hesitated, rehearsing the angles, playing the odds. Would she be home? Would she be willing to talk to me? I was here for Corrina, yes; I owed her something for five hundred bucks. But I was here for myself also, to see Sylvia, to see what I could find out. I had the sense that I was cheating on my client — although, in truth, neither of those words applied. *Cheating? Client?* Both implied a relationship, a sense of connection, that did not exist between Corrina and myself.

The idea was to keep on going, the idea was never to stop. The idea was not to think too much because I knew where thinking led. Standing there, I realized I'd been out, really out — as in, out in a car, out to another neighborhood, to another part of the city, talking to other people — more in the last few days than in all the months before. I felt the tension of it, the anxiety, coat my skin. But that was just the heat, wasn't it? Heat, yes … and all that sweat, a torrent of it, dripping from without and from within.

I rang the doorbell. Again, that sound, like church bells, as if it were announcing the second coming of the Lord. Nothing happened, no clatter of footsteps, no muttering consternation, just a still house on a static afternoon. I waited for a minute, two minutes, wondering if anyone could see me and if so, what they might think. I spun a slow pirouette on the front landing, peering into every copse and corner, but as before, I could see no people anywhere.

Then, over my shoulder, I heard the clicking of the tumbler and felt a blast of cool air at my back. I turned to see the oak door open, that chessboard tiling of the foyer floor. Sylvia was standing before me, dressed in a skirt and strappy sandals; her toes were painted a vermilion red. I felt my breath catch, I wished I hadn't come, all I wanted to do was run away. It was too late for that, though, I was here, and there were things I needed to know.

"Hello," I said.

"It's you." She cut me off, her voice as dry as a canyon fire.

"Yes, I …"

"Did you forget something?'

"No, but —"

"Did my stepdaughter pay you to come back?"

Slowly I nodded, as if I'd been caught at something.

"Another two hundred, or did she raise your rate this time?" She appraised me, flatly, eyes scouring my face. "If this keeps up, I might have to call in the authorities. Wouldn't want you to take advantage of such an impressionable girl."

Impressionable? I almost cried, but before I could, her expression changed. Not softened, exactly, but flattened, grew intrigued. I could see it in her eyes, a subtle glimmer, like there was something here that had to be worked out.

"To hell with it," she said. "It's her lookout. Would you like to come in?"

She ushered me through the foyer and back to the study where we had sat the day before. Had it only been yesterday that I'd been here? It felt like an eternity. I guess that meant I was earning my money — in time, if nothing else. Again, she fixed me a drink and herself a club soda, again she sat across from me. She crossed her legs and smoothed her skirt, as if waiting for me to make the first move.

"I want to ask you about Corrina," I said. "She hasn't told me much, and ..." My voice trailed off.

"You're trying to figure out where you stand."

"Yes, that's it. I mean, you're in a dispute about the will."

"There's no dispute," Sylvia said.

"Wait, what? What about the legal situation?"

"Oh, I expect that it will be adjudicated. But there's no dispute."

I must have looked confused — I was confused — because she took pity on me.

"What I mean," she went on, "is that there's no dispute about the outcome, which is that she's not going to get a dime. I'd take her allowance right now if I could get away with it, but it's all tied up in the estate. Do you know what she does with her money? Have you ever been inside her place?"

I started to say *no*, but it was as if she'd been struck by something, a realization or an idea.

"Wait a minute," she said. "Maybe you can do something for me. You want to know about her, and I need information also …"

Her mouth curled into the most predatory smile I'd ever seen.

"That girl's been trouble since I've known her. Drugs, men, no sense of responsibility. A liar too. She'd steal money out of your wallet right in front of you, then deny it to your face. Have you fucked her? Have you come home to find her in your bed?"

"No," I murmured, "no, it's not like that. I'm not interested in that."

"That's what you say now," she said.

"Really," I replied … although the question lingered. My place was locked, but it wouldn't be hard to gain entry. I didn't even remember if I'd shut the windows before I left. There was nothing to steal, why bother? But then I recalled the searches I had done. I hadn't cleared the history. What if she was looking at my computer right now? The thought electrified me like a bolt of lightning, fusing me to the spot.

"She only came around for money. She'd play off her father's guilt. I'd tell him, she was in her thirties, that she should take care of herself, but he believed he'd clipped her wings."

"Clipped her wings?"

"Not taken care of her enough, or in the right way, while her mother was dying, and then in the years afterwards. Never paid enough attention, he would say, or the proper sort of attention. Always wanted to be somewhere else."

"Was that true?"

"Probably. Not really. What difference does it make anymore? What matters is that she recognized this and used it, used him up. As long as he was living, she treated him like a bank. But what she didn't know was that he'd had enough. He was in the process of changing the will when he died."

"So this is true? She mentioned something, but …"

"But you weren't sure." Sylvia looked at me with satisfaction, as if something had been affirmed. "Yes, it's true, and I'm glad she accepts it. He'd discussed it with his attorney. There was a draft, but he died before the paperwork was finalized."

"Is it possible to see it?"

She laughed, a harsh spray like pebbles against a sheet of glass. "The draft, you mean? No, it is not, although I give you points for asking. You've got guts, which I like. But let's be clear: You're not a cop, you're not anything. You're only here because I'm feeling generous." She paused, took a sip of water, looked at me again. "I will show you something, though, since you seem to want to know."

She stood, smoothed her skirt, ran a hand across her hair, and sidled towards the door.

"If you want another drink," she told me, "help yourself."

I waited for a moment after she left to make sure she wasn't coming back. Then I stood up, left my glass at the bar, took a glance around. In the corner was a desk, bare except for a computer console and keyboard. Without thinking too much about what I was doing, I went around behind it and started opening drawers.

The first two yielded nothing. In the middle drawer, however, I found a zip drive, peeking out from underneath a yellow pad. I picked it up, bounced it in my palm, felt the sharpness of its plastic casing like the blade of a tiny knife. I wondered what, if anything, was on it. Documents, maybe, which could be useful. Or at least informative. I looked at it as if weighing my options. To take it would be stealing. To take it would only further draw me in. Before I could decide, I heard the click of her sandals in the foyer. I shut the drawer and slipped the drive into my pocket, heart beating fast, as if I were on the run. By the time Sylvia re-entered the study, I was standing at the bar, splashing a bit more Maker's into my glass.

"I thought so," she said, almost to herself.

I let the judgment fall from me like water. What did I care what she, what anyone, thought? I took the drink and sat again, eying the manila folder she was holding. She leaned forward, withdrawing a thin sheet of paper, proffering it like some sort of charm. I took it from her. She smiled her Cheshire smile and did not say a word.

The paper was official, a report. Across the top it read: *Application for 72 Hour Detention for Evaluation and Treatment.*

"5150?" I asked.

"Just read."

It had been filled out by a cop, and it was dated from August of last year. It listed Corrina as a potential danger, both to others and to herself. The handwriting was blurry — I was looking at a photocopy of a replicate — but the upshot was that she had been at a party, gotten into a fight. She had ended up threatening to stab the host with a kitchen knife, then locked herself in the bathroom, from which she'd had to be removed, forcibly, by the police.

I tried to remember back to last August, but it was difficult. Had I even noticed her at that point? The address on the form was this one, although that could mean anything. August, August … it was as if the whole year was a blank. Now it was almost August again. I wondered what I would recall in a year.

I handed it back to Sylvia, but she shook her head.

"You can keep it," she said, a little smile flickering on and off across her lips like bad reception. "Maybe it will help in your … *investigation.*"

I wanted to say something, but that zip drive felt like a dead weight in my pocket, and I did not want to tip my hand.

"What you can see, I think," Sylvia continued, "is that she's not stable. She never forgave us for not coming to collect her, for making her stay the full seventy-two hours."

"You didn't get her? You just left her there?"

"What were we supposed to do?" Sylvia asked me. "The first time, we said it was her only get-out-of-jail-free card, that we wouldn't bail her out again."

"The first time?" I could hear the words but couldn't quite follow them.

"Yes, genius, the first time." She spit out another burst of laughter, a harsh and bitter sound. "You want to be a detective? Be a detective. You don't understand what I'm telling you, you're going to need to figure it out."

In my apartment, I tossed the 5150 form and the zip drive on my dresser, went to pour myself a drink. On the way to the kitchen, though, I recalled an echo, a whisper ... *have you come home to find her in your bed?* ... and doubled back my tracks. I looked under the mattress and opened the closet, pawed through the hanging shirts, ran a hand along the upper shelf. Seeing the shovel in its bag made me feel forlorn, but I had no time for that. In the bathroom, I pulled back the curtain on the shower, then examined the kitchen and the living room. My pulse was up: not racing but at a fine high throttle. I checked the windows, made sure they were locked, and pulled the shades. I left the lights off, which rendered the space as a collage of shadows, gray giving way to deeper gray. It was like looking at a time-lapse photo of the last few days, familiar territory blurred to unfamiliar. All the tracks, the pathways, by which I knew myself had been rendered indistinct.

What was I doing? It had started as a favor ... against my better judgment, but nonetheless. I had known she was unbalanced — you could tell that from the screaming — but now the water was becoming deeper in all sorts of ways. Sylvia was giving me the business, she wasn't even trying to be subtle, handing over bits of information while mocking my inability to add them up. And what about the zip drive? What did *it* have to tell me? Would it give me anything I wanted to know?

I returned to the bedroom to retrieve the drive and plugged it into the computer. It took a moment for the icon to appear. The drive bore no identification, just a manufacturer's brand. On it, I found a single folder, which held a dozen jpegs. The images were numbered, but none of them were named.

I decided to look at them in sequence. I don't know what I was expecting, but when I clicked on the first image, I found myself submerging once again. The photo was of Corrina's father; I recognized him from the photo in the *Times*. He was naked, fitted with a ball gag, bound in kneeling position on a bed. The second introduced Sylvia, in a mask and corset, cat-o'-nine-tails in her hand. It was hard to make out her eyes. In the third, she was whipping him. The rest unfolded as a progression: close-up of his buttocks, latticed with stripes of red like laces, another of his face, arranged in a rictus of excitation, if not exactly pain. I wanted to see his eyes, but they were shut; his mouth, however, even with the gag in place, was upturned in a smile. Looking at him, I was flooded with rage. What a fucking amateur. He was having too much fun, playing at degradation. He didn't understand that the point was the humiliation and the shame. I knew more than a little bit about that. I wanted to feel bad, although mostly I didn't feel at all. As for this, it was all so clinical, so scripted, so vanilla — this scroll of photos, one after another, arranged into a narrative I could make sense of, and then, perhaps, make go away. I skimmed through the remaining images; the only surprise came in the last one. There, his face looked like he was being throttled, as if he could barely breathe.

What did I make of it? And what should I do with the zip drive, now that it was here? It was evidence, of course, but of what? I couldn't say. And I was going to have to return it, that much was clear, before she noticed it was gone. Idly, without any real intention, I copied the images to my hard drive.

And I don't know what I was thinking, or if I was

thinking anything at all. And I don't know if it had anything to do with the drinking, although I'd been drinking slowly, steadily, all day. I unplugged the drive and stashed it, along with the 5150, in the top drawer of my dresser, beneath the socks and underwear. Then I went online, searching out other images like those I'd seen. It grew dark while I was looking, gray evaporating into blackness, the only light the glow from my screen. As it happens, there were a number of fetish sites catering to this kind of thing. As it happens? As I already knew. Yes, but I had never paid that much attention. I didn't share this particular predilection; my tastes were more … particular, I guess you'd call them. Specialized. My tastes … some of them, there were no websites for. Mostly, they took place in solitude, release as a matter of mind and not of body, which was the nature of the internet as well. Finally, I found a site with a members' community, to which I uploaded the images for public view.

I knew it was wrong, what I was doing. I knew it wasn't good for me. I knew there was no place for it, that this was not how civilized people behaved. I knew it opened me to danger, not physical danger, although maybe, but danger of the spirit, of the soul. And yet, what did those words mean? *Civilized? Soul?* They were like telegrams from another century. I didn't believe in them, didn't see the point. It was all something to put on, like my suit and my red tie. *Civilized* like what? Like a mansion in Benedict Canyon with a wood-grained study that looked like something from a movie and your bedroom games upstairs? *Soul* like what? Like the torment of screaming yourself to sleep? No, this was a challenge, a provocation. This was peeling back the surface to reveal the tumult underneath.

There was something else, too, but I couldn't put my finger on it — at least, that is, until I cycled through the images a final time. In a few, Corrina's father was alone, but most showed him and Sylvia. And then it hit me: if they were both in the frame, who was shooting the picture? It could have been a timed release, but that didn't seem correct. Something about the angles, which shifted from shot to shot as if the camera were hand-held. I scrolled through the images again, looking for a clue. I enlarged those shots, leaned in close to the screen of my computer. It felt as if I were the one who was making the pictures, head under the photographer's hood of some ancient camera and all of us in a studio somewhere. Surely, that had happened; I'd seen old photographic porn, some going back as far as the 1850s, all those young bodies twisting in and out of all the familiar contortions, except that they and everyone who had ever known them was now forever dead. When we looked at such images, historical or current, we always thought about what was in the frame, not who was standing behind the lens. This photographer, though, whoever he or she might be, was a key part of the mix. How would I find out? I didn't have a notion, except for the growing awareness that I was in over my head.

I shut the computer and came out of the bedroom. I felt unsettled, raw. I opened the curtains and stood in the darkness looking across the courtyard; Corrina's apartment was dark as well. Slowly, silently, I edged open the windows. The air felt tepid, hardly moving — the same, inside and out.

I turned my back, refreshed my drink, sat down without turning on the lights. After a while, I got up to go to the bathroom. When I came back, the woman across the courtyard had started screaming again.

QUESTION NUMBER FIVE:
DON'T GIVE ME NO JIVE?

It might have been that I was looking to get back at everyone, or that I didn't care. It might have been that I was trying to trace the line between reality and imagination. Or trying to blur that line. What were those pictures? Would anybody notice them? On the one hand, they were as real as it got, photographic images, undoctored, or so it appeared. What they portrayed, what they captured, had actually taken place. On the other, they were mediated, poses, Sylvia and her husband playing yet another set of roles. As to whether, or what, roles they played when they were not in front of a camera ... well, I didn't know enough to say.

And what about the shooter? Accomplice or participant? The question made me want to go back up the hill to Sylvia's and make a thorough search, although I knew I would do no such thing. That would require planning, cunning, subterfuge, and if anything, what I was discovering was just how little I knew to do.

Yes, how little, and in every area. I had accepted seven hundred dollars because it seemed like free money, like a stipend for going along. The stakes were real, sure they were, thirty million dollars, but what did that mean to me? Nothing, a lark, a role, a fantasy, something to fill the lonely hours, something to make the time pass. What did it matter whether Corrina or Sylvia got the money? What did it matter that they couldn't share? What did it matter that I was suspended somehow in between them, drawn in by one, turned by the other, a piece in a game only they knew how to play?

No, I thought, sitting in the still air of the living room, making so little noise, so little movement, I couldn't even say I was alive. I kept the lights out, listening as the night began to settle, the sound of traffic hissing past on Franklin Avenue, the sound of Corrina's shrieking as it subsided into sobs. Was I the only one, I wondered, who noticed? Was I the only one who was disturbed? It had to be that way, didn't it? All of us so jaded that it didn't matter, that we barely heard her anymore? Look at me — I wasn't doing anything and I knew her, I was working for her, I was the keeper of her secrets in my way. Keeper of her secrets, yes, although at least one was a secret she hadn't shared. Unless … unless … unless what? I couldn't put my finger on it, but there was something in the screaming, her behavior, that I didn't understand. Complicity? That might be it. But complicity between whom and whom?

The truth was that I was now complicit with both Corrina and Sylvia, that I had a foot in each camp. Each camp? More like in each closet, in each bedroom, in each hidden, secret drawer. There was more to be exposed, I understood that, just as I understood that I would only find what they wanted me to find. I was already past the point of control, at the mercy of their whims, just as I had been in my marriage, just as I had been in everything.

My marriage … I wanted to stay away from that, I didn't want to fall into the past. Everything depended on remaining present, on distracting myself from what I knew or had been, from what I had done or where I'd gone. My wife: where she was now? Better to forget I'd ever known her, that she had ever occupied my imagination or my heart. But when I closed my eyes, her face rose up unbidden, like a rancid rose. Not just any face, but her face with that man behind her, the fulfillment of her fantasy. The turning point? Perhaps, although in fact, there was no turning point, there never is. Just a series of decisions made — or more often left unmade, a going with the flow. I was titillated, I'll admit it, by her talk, her wild ways. Titillated until the time came to take things further, when titillation yielded to despair. I had been complicit in that too, although the joke, it turned out, was on me. And the thing was that I didn't even know it, that I didn't even know myself.

That was the part I couldn't process, that I had been so wrong, so fucking clueless, about everything I was.

Still, even now, I found myself stirred up. I could feel the weight of it, my desire and my degradation, the physical pull like a heaviness below the belt. I could feel my resistance wavering. I didn't want to do this anymore. And yet, who cared, really, what I did or what I didn't? Who cared what I had or I had not? I was just another organism, unknown, unnoticed, flesh already rotting from the dissolution that was to come.

Without turning on the lights, I got up and slipped into the bedroom. I logged into the website where I had posted the images from the zip drive. They weren't what I was looking for, but before I could click though to search for other images, I found myself confronting something that froze the breath inside my chest. There they were, Sylvia and her husband, one of the images I had posted, high on the homepage, featured slot. I reloaded the page to be sure, but it remained the same. Someone had added a tag or headline, but I didn't pay attention to that. No, what mattered were the numbers: the photo already had more than a thousand likes.

I had to return the drive, that was the main thing. Before Sylvia discovered it was gone. I went to the window, but Corrina's place was dark, and silent now. The sky had darkened also — full dark now, no stars — or maybe it just looked that way through the filter of the city's night-time glow.

I had no way to get in touch with Sylvia, but that didn't matter. This was a problem with only one solution: if I wanted to sneak the drive back, I would have to take it there myself. And why not? Sylvia had told me I could help her. I could use that to try, once more, to talk my way inside. I could say I was concerned about Corrina, that things sounded as if they were going around the bend. Although for the moment, I couldn't hear her, I had no doubt that she'd start screaming soon again. With any luck, I'd be out of here by that point, on my way back up the hill, or anywhere, in a different, better world than this.

I shut the computer. With the curtains closed and the night outside, it was as if existence had fallen away. I remembered, as a kid, feeling safe in small, dark places, as if, were I to crawl deep enough, I could evade the prying eyes of God. Maybe it would be enough to make that motherfucker forget me, to protect me and make time stop. The smaller the space the better, the fewer windows, the more silent and still the air. It was as if I had removed myself. It was as if I had been erased.

What to do? The decision was mine. Not that it had ever been any different, from the moment I'd let Corrina into the apartment that first time. I turned on the light and rummaged for dark pants, a pullover, gloves. I grabbed a pair of sneakers, laced them to my feet. In the mirror, I looked like some sort of half-assed hipster, all shadows and straight lines. I slipped the zip drive in my pocket, and eased out of the apartment, following the pathway out to Franklin, where I linked to Lyft and waited for my ride.

Again, I had the driver drop me off before we reached the house, about half a mile down the hill. I waited until his taillights had evaporated like bubbles in a champagne glass before I began the climb. There was not a lot of traffic, and each time I heard an engine rising, I would duck my head, turn away from the road. I still didn't know what I was doing, but when had I ever known what I was doing? If I knew what I was doing, I wouldn't be dressed in dark colors, contemplating … what? a break-in? some kind of confrontation? I had no idea what I would find.

The night was quiet, cooling, but I was overheating. Not from the exertion — or not completely — but from everything surrounding it. Whatever I had done in my life, it did not include this. I had never stolen anything, never had to return it, never skulked around the edges of another person's home, like a stalker in some bad TV show. Everything I knew came from some other source:

the dark clothes, the silence, the sheath of night. Playing a part, pawn in the game … and yet, whose game was I playing? My own game now. This was my choice, although what I was choosing I could not explain. I kept my head down, mounted the slope of the road. The air bore the faintest breath of smoke. The houses were set back mostly, behind hedges and long lawns; the light that came through their windows did not make it to the street. Up ahead, Sylvia's pile sat dark in the gloom of evening, like some sort of wreck, some sort of ruin, more archaeological site than home.

When I got to her driveway, I paused, listening to the water running in the fountain. I felt like a memory come alive. The house was quiet and shuttered. I wasn't sure what I should do. If I'd had a number, I might have been tempted to call it. But Corrina was right, that would be stupid: to leave such a fingerprint. The surveillance state, that was its biggest betrayal, not that we were watched by the government (when had we not been watched by the government?) but that we now watched ourselves. It was nearly impossible to remain unnoticed, although the paradox, I hoped, was that this made us more anonymous still. How to sort through all the information? How to assess it, how to know? I took a perverse comfort from this — or was it self-justification? — reassured that whatever I did, whatever I bought or posted, I was too small to notice. It was the virtual version of hiding in small rooms. I had known people who felt the opposite, who craved surveillance, as if the eye of God were looking down to keep them safe. I did not share that feeling. I couldn't imagine that God gave a shit, except, perhaps, to fuck with me. At best, I wanted to believe that God, or the universe, was indifferent. I wanted to believe it wasn't interested at all. I wanted to believe that God, if it existed, had more important issues. I wanted to believe that God, if it existed, had created us and then moved on. I wasn't sure about any of it, except that often the universe felt actively malevolent. But either way, God was not on our side. This is what people didn't want to face, that the universe was cold, was

57

isolating if it was anything, that we lived and died for no reason, that nobody was coming to help us, that nobody was keeping score.

I took a quick look around, rotating my head like a periscope. Here too, nobody, no one on the grounds. I slipped onto the low expanse of the front lawn, forcing myself to keep my movements contained and small, not to break into a run. Now that I was here, I felt anonymity desert me; it occurred to me, for the first time and all of a sudden, that I had no idea what protections were in place. There could be cameras, sensors, already a message could be pulsing to some security office, cars dispatched, officers en route. For a moment, I almost turned back, but it was too late. If there were cameras, my image had been captured, so there was nothing left to do. I felt better once I got to the house, where I clung to the walls like a shadow, disembodied, as if I were somewhere else. That's how it felt, too, like being in a dream or some sort of video game, like being manipulated from the outside. I knew better than to try the front door, but after I caught my breath and quieted the ringing thrum of blood behind my forehead, I mounted the steps and tried the handle anyway. It was locked, and behind its leaded panes, I could see nothing, only opaque gray. Did she know about the zip drive? Was she waiting for me in there? Did she have someone with her or was she alone? For a moment, the image of her in that getup, garters and corset, burst into my brain as if it had been burnt there, and I felt the jolt push through my body, an electric pulse. *Not now,* I thought, *pay attention* — although wasn't that the problem, that I hadn't paid attention *enough?*

I moved around the side of the house and into the backyard. Here, a long veranda and a wall of picture windows, with French doors opening into a vast living room. I pressed my face against the glass, trying to imagine the layout inside. I could see another set of French doors along the other wall, which clearly led into the entry foyer. The room was a reminder of everything that separated us — not just its size and comfort (two couches, a pair of wing chairs with ottomans, all arranged around a coffee table as big as a sedan), but also the fact that she had never let me see it, never let me know that it was there. It was as if I weren't worthy or important. For a moment, this got my hackles up; who was she to judge? It would be a mistake to under-estimate me. But then I remembered where I was, on the outside looking in, always on the outside looking in, with no plan to gain access, no plan for anything at all. Un-derestimating? What was there to underestimate? I was no formidable adversary. Standing here as the night grew deeper, I had to reckon with a bleak realization: that I was no adversary at all.

I had been hoping for an open window, a breach, the sort of carelessness I imagined might mark the mon-strously wealthy, who smashed up things and creatures and then retreated back into their money or their vast carelessness or whatever it was that kept them together, and let other people clean up the mess they had made. But that was a false illusion, wasn't it, like so much of what I wanted to believe. Sylvia was the opposite of careless, she was calculating, cunning, mapping out the angles, de-ciding which to play. She had her stepdaughter dead to rights, although there was something missing, something under the surface, something between the two of them that I had yet to see. And she had me also, had me where she wanted me, up in the air, confused, off-balance, acting stupid. I was the careless one, not she.

Careless? Yes, for what else could you call it, my decision to come here without a plan? I had the sense, standing on her veranda beneath a darkness thick as death that I was sinking in the ocean, that all this sky was water, rising over me. It was deep, which made it hard to see, no light penetrating anywhere. I could sense that there were dangers, but I didn't know what or where they were. And the weight of it, the pressure of all those cubic feet of hy-drogen and oxygen, was forcing whatever air remained out of my chest.

I tried to calm myself, but my heart was racing. I went into a crouch, head in my hands. I breathed, slowly, in and out in and out, the rhythm like a mantra, the silence like a scream. I needed to get out of here, but what would I do with that zip drive? How would I get it back? I thought about just dropping it on the veranda or by the front door, but that would be the wrong move. Especially if there were surveillance cameras, it would only point the finger back at me.

I breathed again, felt the panic recede a little. It was still there, but not quite at the point of seizing, and I was able to make a quick inventory of the house. It was vast, three storeys, with eaves and wings and outcroppings, like a cliff face or a set of peaks. I had not expected there to be any points of entry on the ground floor, but if an upper window were ajar, I had imagined I might be able to get inside that way. The second and third floors, however, presented a face as closed and nondescript as the one I wished to present to the world. I forced myself to continue circling, remaining always in the shadows, slow and silent, attuned to every step. Nothing, not a breach or a gap or any point of ingress. It was a fully armored skin. I paused when I came to the study, which I could see through panes of leaded manor glass. Inside, among the shadows, were the club chairs where I had sat with her, and the square shape of the desk. I pushed against the windows, but they didn't even rattle. There was no give. I scanned the corners of the landscaped yard for a rock but the property was manicured … and anyway that, too, would defeat the purpose, obliterate my efforts to go unobserved.

So I made the only choice that was available to me. I turned around and headed home. Back around to the front of the house and across the driveway, and out to Benedict Canyon Drive, which I followed down, a mile or so until I got to Sunset and the Beverly Hills Hotel. I walked into the Polo Lounge as if I were a guest and asked for a Maker's on the rocks. When I was finished, I asked for another one. Then, I ordered a Lyft and went out front to wait for it, that zip drive as heavy in my pocket as an anchor or an albatross.

The apartment was quiet when I got back. The night had settled into stunted stillness and there was a slight breeze blowing, not cool exactly, but calming, a caress. I let myself in, tossed my keys on the coffee table, didn't switch on the lights. I wasn't hiding, no point in hiding now since I wasn't going anywhere, but I wanted to remain in darkness, a shadow or a wraith. In the dark, it was as if I weren't really present; in the dark, it was as if I had never been. I, me, myself, and everyone else; in the dark it was as if we had all been eclipsed. There was nothing here except perception, dissolving into particles, the peculiar, collage-like effect of lack of light. The darkness was so thick, it felt like a curtain, which meant I had to reach my hand in front of me to part it, to clear a space, a passage, for myself.

Quietly, I felt my way to the kitchen, found a bottle of Maker's in the cabinet, poured a glass. I took a sip, felt the breeze infiltrate the windows, which I had left open to the night. The liquor seeped through me like molasses, from the shoulders down. I felt a loosening, a thickening, as if my limbs had been immersed in jelly, a flush of something — heat — in the cooling, as if there were no barrier any longer between inside and out. I settled in the chair, took a deep breath, closed my eyes. When I opened them, I could make out the details of the room. Dark shapes, blunt: the counter, the couch, the table, all hulking in the grayness, as if they had been molded out of clay. It was like a surrealist installation, the edges loose and not quite defined, specific and archetypal all at once. Like the veil had been pulled back on the world and what I saw now was the elemental, Plato's cave, the borders pushed, the boundaries blurred, and me here, all alone, with little sense of my body, as if I were dissolving in the night.

Then, out of the corner of my ear I heard it, a whisper or a creak. It sounded like bedsprings, like it was coming from inside the house. All of a sudden, I could hear Sylvia's voice in my head, as clear as if she were speaking: *Have you come home to find her in your bed?* And how had I answered? *No*, I'd told her, *I'm not interested —*

but even though I'd checked the apartment that day upon returning, the truth was that I hadn't quite believed what she'd said. *How?* I thought, but the answer was right in front of me, those windows I'd left open. It was as if I'd given her an invitation, an invitation to trespass, to cross the line, to collapse the distance, to eradicate the space between. Hadn't that been the idea all along? She was trying to draw me in. She and her stepmother, the two of them, birds of a feather. I wished I'd never gotten involved. I wished I hadn't answered the door that first night. Or that I had sent her on her way. Now, however, it was too late for wishes. Now had come the time for truth.

I finished my drink and set the glass down. I unlaced my sneakers, took them off. I walked in slow steps toward the bedroom. The door was three-quarters closed. Gently, I pushed against it; it opened in a silent sweep. There on the bed was a shape underneath a sheet that glowed white in the darkness, and protruding from it was Corrina's head. I had hoped to catch her unaware, unguarded, but she was watching out for me.

"I thought you'd never come in here," she said, and then she pushed the sheet aside and she was naked except for her ankle boots, legs spread just a little, darkness yielding to a deeper darkness and nowhere for me to rest my eyes.

"What are you doing? Put that sheet back on."

"You're going to have to make me," she giggled, her breath so thick with alcohol that I could smell it from across the room.

"What do you like?" she went on. "I bet you're into all sorts of dirty things."

On the dresser, my laptop sat mute like a witness. It was closed, but that didn't mean a thing. For a moment, I felt a flash of panic, but it receded when she put her right hand between her legs. At first, I thought it was for show, but it wasn't long before I realized there was nothing showy about it. She ground against the mattress, rubbing vigorously. "Come over here," she groaned, tongue flicking in and out of her mouth. When I didn't, she moved to the edge of the mattress. It was just a matter of time before she made herself cum in my bed.

"Come over here," she said again, words slurring into moans more than syllables. She buckled, then rose upright again, her body its own surging force. I stayed where I was, as if paralyzed, as if this were a trap. I couldn't take my eyes away: the swell of her breasts, the curve of her shoulders, the blurring movement of her fingers, those boots and her gasping, ragged breath. I could feel myself getting pulled in as if she were a magnet. But I knew that once I got to that bed, it would be done. I would have made a choice, I would have chosen a side, allowed myself to be drawn more fully into something I didn't want, allowed myself to be seduced. At the same time, another part of me was wondering if this was even real. Could it be that she was just another tulpa, a projection, an invention of my mind? The look on her face was one of abandonment, but it also looked like she was working hard. Working hard to carry this off, to throw me out of balance, to bring herself off not as she might do in private but as a provocation or attack. What did she want? I couldn't figure out the angle. Pretty soon, I wasn't sure I'd care. Suddenly, she looked right at me. Her eyes were piercing, sharp and blue. I felt them cut me, felt a jolt of electricity pass between us and settle in my solar plexus. For a moment, we just stared at one another as the room grew still. In the silence, she growled, a guttural wail. Then, she stopped and grunted, in a voice as pointed as an order: "I paid you. Seven hundred dollars. You belong to me." Her hand began to move again. "Now get over here and fuck me. Like a good employee. Get over here and do what you are told."

I wish I could say that I turned around, that I dragged her from the bed. I wish I could say that I threw her into the courtyard drunk and disorderly and naked, that I exposed her in her shame. I wish I could say these things, but this is not what occurred. No, something about her words, their tone of degradation, penetrated me. It was as she had become my wife in all her wildness, or Sylvia, in her dominatrix getup, taking me with no remorse. It was as if I had been exposed, or even worse, seen — shamed, revealed to the very essence of my core. I knew this feeling, and I liked it. I had craved it for so long. And now here I was, moving on the tulpa, on Corrina, tumbling out of my pants, my shirt, stumbling in my insistence, my desire. I couldn't reach her fast enough. I fell and had to crawl. And it was crawling that I came to her, and it was crawling that I came upon her, and then rose up to embrace her — no, not to embrace her but to be consumed by her, as if this were not sex but an inferno, and she were not a woman but a raging fire.

When I awoke, we were still in darkness, but I could feel her body next to mine. Smooth, warm, no longer a flame but a smoldering set of embers, although I no longer wanted to play with fire. My mouth was parched, as if I'd been encased in dirt, as if I had been buried alive. Naked, I went into the kitchen and poured a glass of water, stood at the window staring into the empty courtyard as I drank it down.

Back in the bedroom, I noticed something glinting on the shaded surface of the floor. It was the zip drive; it must have fallen from my pocket in my rush to get undressed. *Fuck*, I thought, *I'm glad she didn't see this* ... and now I was remembering my misbegotten trip into the canyon, the impenetrability of all those walls. How was I going to get this back to Sylvia without her noticing?

How was I to obviate my guilt?

I could always throw the drive away, I guessed, and plead ignorance if I were asked. It wouldn't be the first time I had deflected trouble with a lie. Then I caught sight of Corrina's purse, a small black leather backpack that fastened with a snap. It lay on the floor next to her balled up jeans. I looked to the bed; her chest moved up and down in easy intervals, her limbs strewn wide like scattered sticks. I coughed, once and again, a little louder, just to test it ... she did not stir. Slowly, almost in stop-motion, I picked up the drive and slipped it in the center section of the backpack. I pushed it down and shifted the other contents — wallet, a compact, lipstick — until it could not be seen. I waited for a moment and another, breathing quietly but deeply, trying to align my inhalations with hers. When I got back in bed, I made sure not to brush against her. I fell into a dreamless sleep.

In the morning, when I awakened, Corrina was gone. I lifted my head, but there was nothing: no pictures, no handbag, not even the impression of her head upon the pillow.

It was as if she had dissolved from a dream into a dream.

QUESTION NUMBER SIX:
HOW LONG TO GET FIXED?

I didn't see Corrina for a few days. It was as if, having come and having gone, she had dissolved. But I couldn't stop thinking about her. Not about what had happened, although that too, its implications. But even more, the zip drive, sitting in her purse like a hand grenade, ready to go off. I had pulled the pin, gotten her involved, implicated in my little conspiracy. I was acting on impulse, yet my impulses ... I couldn't say what they were. It was like a *pas de trois*, this awkward dance among Corrina, Sylvia, and myself. And still, I couldn't explain my presence. Seven hundred dollars? Was this a fair price for my complicity?

I kept waiting, waiting for Corrina, waiting for a knock on the door. I sat inside my apartment like a spider, doing nothing, saying nothing, no idea how to act. Every couple of hours I logged onto that website, where the photos had receded after their initial rush. Thrill of the new ... but the truth was they weren't so new, weren't so titillating, nothing like the other images, the videos, in which men and women exposed themselves in ways that made it hard to imagine that they were really living, that they could go to work, greet their neighbors, walk into a hotel bar and order a drink. It was only skin-deep, I guess, but it felt much deeper, watching them revealed. My favorites were the most homemade, the least polished, in which real people, overweight, no silicone, tangled with one another on small beds with dirty sheets. What were they doing? It wasn't the money, there was no money in it, and it couldn't be attention or fame. It was something else, something deeper, pathological, as if I were looking at their psyches turned inside out. The same, I suppose, might be said of me, but I wasn't in any photos and I would never be. Even with my wife, we had acted out our fantasies in private, or semi-private. We had left no visible, no discoverable, trace. What made someone unveil themselves on the internet, naked, fucking, penetrated — physically, spiritually — in every way you could imagine, and some that you could not? It was as if daily life were not enough, as if they, as if all of us, had grown so numbed that the only way to feel anything any longer was by stripping away every last defense, every last bit of propriety, even (or especially) their shame.

And yet, where did that leave me, checking on the photos I had posted, wondering when the other shoe would drop? Where did that leave me, with the memory of Corrina, the shame and thrill of it, of her telling me that I'd been bought and sold? In the dark that night, I had imagined, more than once, that she was Sylvia, had lost myself until the two of them blurred together in my mind. *Sylvia*, I had whispered in my head, and if I did not speak those syllables aloud, I had the sense Corrina would not mind. There were layers here, layers of humiliation, or maybe it was just the humiliation of being alive. Either way, I was in it now, with ramifications, a storm of fallout gathering around my head. If I'd had a car, I might have gone on a long drive. That was something I had once liked to do. But it took all the energy I could muster just to sit upright. The heat was so oppressive, I could barely make myself put on clothes.

Then, the screaming started up again. I wasn't sure how long it had been, two nights, maybe three, but I could hear it through the windows in the living room. Just another evening. Just another part of the scenery, the price of living in the complex, and who was to say that she was wrong? I felt like screaming also, not just tonight but many nights, and if I didn't ... well, that didn't mean I had self-control. I was adrift too, adrift in a different way, shuttered and silent, disconnected and remote. I didn't see the point any more than she did, none of this made sense to me. One day I would be dead and none of it would matter, just as none of it mattered now. It was what drove me nuts about people, their desperate hope, their insistence that there was more than this, like a fairy tale they told themselves. It didn't lead to anything and it never would, no matter how many lies we wanted to believe. Save the planet, don't save the planet … but the planet didn't need saving, and as for us, salvation was never in the cards. God wasn't love either, but thanks for playing. God was a disrupter or God was inaccessible. Or it wasn't anything at all.

I listened to the throaty oscillation of her wailing, rising and falling like the call of some exotic bird. It was different tonight, not in intonation but in timbre, or maybe it's that she seemed to be screaming out a word. In the past, her moaning had been low, inexplicable, indistinct as anything but pain. This was more directed, as if she were shrieking at someone. For a moment, I wondered if she were alone. Then, the night reconfigured in a shape of stunning clarity. It was not a word she kept repeating, it was a name. She was calling it over and over, as if she were in an argument — as if she were fighting someone off. I crept closer to the window. *Sylvia?* No, it was not Sylvia, those were not the syllables I was hearing.

It was my name that filled the air.

At first, I thought about doing nothing, but I knew that wasn't going to work. I lived here, and if I didn't know my neighbors, this was still too close to home. I had no choice but to wade in deeper, I had no choice but to engage. This was why I didn't get involved with people: too much drama, too many opportunities to be betrayed. I wanted to hide, to wait my time out on the planet, to be as indistinct, as nondescript as I could. I wanted to do what I had to do, nothing more, to live and die like an allegation or a rumor. Or not even — to be overlooked. I wanted to drink my whiskey, dream my dreams, and rot from the inside out. I didn't believe in corruption because of course we were all already corrupted; it came with the territory, it was both a state of matter and a state of being.

"Fuck," I said and slipped on my shoes. I stepped outside, glanced at the other units. Nearly every window was dark. That didn't mean anything, mine had been dark also, but it felt reassuring, as if I were invisible. Quickly, I cut across the courtyard. On her step, the hibachi was filled with half-burnt coals and bore the faintest breath of lighter fluid. Behind it, her door stood ajar. I pushed against it, just a little, and it opened further to reveal an apartment that was a mirror image of mine. Mirror? Hah, I thought, that was a joke. Inverse image was more like it, ego to my id. The living room looked like a showroom or a stage set; it looked like a demonstration unit. There were three matching couches, although two, technically, were loveseats. But it didn't matter because none of them appeared to have been used. They were blue velvet, puffed and empty, with throw pillows arranged at precise angles, like the formal living room I'd seen through the windows of Sylvia's house. This room, too, was centered by a coffee table, although a fraction of the size — square and wooden, with a glass top and underneath it, a recessed shelf for books or magazines. A pair of matching end tables flanked the longer sofa, each topped by a Tiffany-style lamp. The lights were off, but I could make out the shapes if not the details, thanks to the diffuse glow from the open door. In the dimness, I could see framed art on the walls, reproductions or originals, although the images were difficult to decipher.

Or maybe I just didn't want to know.

This wasn't what I'd anticipated when Sylvia had asked if I'd seen Corrina's apartment. If I'd thought about it at all, I would have imagined a place that looked as if it had been tossed, as if it had been ransacked, that was as disordered as the space inside her mind. I would have imagined something unclean: clothes in piles, dirty dishes everywhere. A display as unfettered as the way she carried herself, the way she had laid claim to my living room. This, however … this was like an empty spirit. This was like a body without a soul. I was in a room that contained no evidence it had ever been occupied by a human being.

I was alone, that was the other thing, and I wasn't sure what I should make of it, whether I should feel relieved or more disturbed. No Corrina, not in *here*, even as I could still hear the rising and the falling of her wails. I knew where she was, although I wasn't sure I wanted to make the long walk to her bedroom. Or what she might be doing once I did. I kept flashing back to the night inside my apartment. I didn't want to go through that again.

And yet, here I was and what choice did I have? I can't go on, I'll go on, and so I stood for a moment gathering my breath before doubling back to close the front door, cutting myself off from the world and its ... what? Clarity?

No, only a different kind of madness, or perhaps a more effective mask.

I crossed the living room at its edges, not wanting to disturb the scene. Even my presence, my breathing, felt like an intrusion, an assault on the sterility. As I moved, I caught more details: a vintage deco cocktail cabinet with cut crystal decanters, a filigreed standing lamp. The bedroom door was closed and I listened at the threshold. For a moment, I wondered if she knew I was here. Through the wood, I could hear her sobbing, or coming down off sobbing. It sounded as if she were settling. I remembered my wife like this, the last few weeks or months before we separated, after it became apparent to both of us that we had poisoned whatever it was we thought we'd shared. Poison. We'd been young, incautious, we'd fallen prey to our desires. Or no, not our desires, our darkness, some line within us, within each of us, that we felt impelled to cross. This is what madness is, I think, this impulse to the precipice, for there's a precipice in every one of us. The death instinct, Freud called it, as in: *opposition between the ego or death instincts and the sexual or life instincts*, although in my experience, the two are not opposed. Aligned, more like it, sex and self-destruction, breath and death. Just look at where I was right now.

Right now ... right now. Right now, the only thing to do was go through the bedroom door and face whatever was waiting on the other side of it, sex or death or some new form of degradation and despair. I turned the handle slowly. The lights were out in here as well, and all the colors bleached towards gray.

Again, night coalesced in little particles, like some pointillist landscape in black and white. I blinked, I wasn't sure what I was seeing. The room was empty, except for a mattress, on which there were clothes or blankets stacked. No illusions here, no stage set, no impression of an ordered life. No sign of Corrina either, until I noticed the blankets heaving and understood that she was underneath. Here we were again, in the same room, and she had no idea.

"Corrina?" I said, my voice soft. From under the blankets, I could hear her moan. "Corrina? Why don't you come out so I can see you? Can I turn on a light?"

"NO!" she shrieked, casting the blanket aside as if she were emerging from a spell. She came up then, a swimmer surfacing, eyes wild, cheeks streaked with snot and tears and mascara, hands balled into fists. She was dressed, jeans and a tee shirt, although the shirt glowed wet with something viscous. Her feet were bare. "I don't want you here. This is my apartment. Get out."

I didn't say anything at first. I didn't know what to say. I had an idea that she had found the zip drive, but I didn't want to commit.

"What is it?" I asked finally, modulating my voice to sound as if I cared. All I cared about was learning what was what. It had been capricious, idiotic, first stealing that drive and then posting those images before discarding the evidence in her purse. Three steps, the rule of three, to rack and ruin.

"I thought I could trust you, I thought ..." She went silent for a moment before letting out another scream. This one was quieter, though, undifferentiated; it did not include my name. The sound was of an engine running out of gas, energy dissipating towards entropy.

"Trust me how?" I asked, a little trepidatious. It felt like walking across a field of ordnance, as if any second I could blow myself up on a mine.

"Trust you, trust you. How could you do this to me?"

"I haven't done anything. I heard you shouting and I wanted to be sure you were okay."

71

I could sense her looking at me, although the room was too dark, really, to tell. The moment stretched like taffy, like a chaw of bubble gum. She was bouncing lightly on her haunches, as if preparing to spring. I felt myself withdrawing, backing to the door. What if she came at me? I hadn't thought of her as a physical threat, but now I wasn't sure. She had broken into my apartment, hadn't she, which was its own sort of aggression, and as for what had happened afterwards … well, that was an aggression of a different kind. There had been a moment, in the bed, when she had grabbed my head and forced it into the mattress. Then she had spanked me — not hard but hard enough. What had she said? I couldn't quite remember, didn't want to remember, but it had something to do with paying for the privilege of doing what she would. I didn't think so, but I didn't protest; there was something thrilling about the moment, the sense that anything might go. It had been so long since I'd done anything like that, since I'd let everything slide out of control. All those weeks and months, numbing desire, memory, with alcohol, all those weeks and months of trying to erase myself. It may be true that all of us will be erased, but we can do a lot of damage before we go. I know, I have caused my share, more than my share, I have my sins to be accounted for. This was what I was doing in my apartment, paying a kind of penance, and it was also, I thought now, what I was doing here.

I waited to see what might be coming. I waited, but nothing was. We watched each other, two wary animals caught together in a lair. We were circling, or waiting to be circled. We were mapping out the choreography, or at least I thought she was. As for me, there was nothing, just a blankness. For no reason, a piece of music started to assert itself, and before I knew what I was doing, I began to sing.

Corrine, Corrina, where you been so long?

I never took my eyes from her. That thin and lilting

melody drifted through the room like a wisp of smoke, barely apprehended before it was gone. The tension grew. It was not unbearable; no, the opposite, oddly pleasing, like the moment right before you fall asleep. At some point there would need to be a release or a reckoning, a falling backwards into something else. I recognized that, but I didn't know what it would look like. I watched and I waited, wondering what would happen next.

Except that when it happened, the next thing, I wasn't ready. When it happened, it caught me by surprise. Corrina rose up on the bed like a ghoul, like a specter. In the darkness, it was as if she had become both shade and shadow, growing to encompass every wall. I watched the blackness spread, a rushing torrent, like the aftermath of an eclipse. Just as it appeared to reach me, she fell back. It was like watching a building collapse in slow motion — first her head, then her arms across her body, grasping her chest and shoulders in a tight X. Her knees bent and her back bowed, and with a low moan that sounded less animal than mechanical, she slipped to the floor beside the bed.

"Corrina?" I whispered. No response. Silence filled the room like ash. I could barely feel my feet, barely feel the floor beneath them as I floated to the bed. She lay crumpled, body folded in upon itself like a pile of rags.

"Corrina?" I said again, and reached out a hand. As my fingers brushed her shoulders, she convulsed. One big shudder, and a second, smaller one, and then she was wailing, "No, no, no, don't touch me" … her head shaking back and forth.

And I might have said, *let me help you.* And I might have said, *let's get you back in bed.* That's how it's supposed to go, isn't it, when the bad crazies take hold of you and all you want is someone to take care of the details, smooth your hair against your forehead, tell you everything will be all right? But how could I, how could that happen? I was the catalyst. First, I had given in to her, then I'd slipped that zip drive in her purse. I'd left her with the evidence, left her holding the bag. She knew it, she had to, that must be what this was about. And yet, what was there to do? Nothing, just keep playing dumb and let her … what? Think I was gaslighting her? But how did you gaslight someone who was already gaslighting herself?

Or was I the one who was being gaslighted?

The thought made me stop and look, really look at her, as much as I could see between the grains of night. Her body huddled, like a scarecrow fallen, sack of bones and hair and skin. Unlike a scarecrow, though, she was crusty with the thick, rich scent of her effluvia. Unlike a scarecrow, she was living — or at least she was awake. There was something rank about her, unwashed, something feral or elemental: a scent, a spoor, a trace of scat by which she might be tracked. I wondered when she'd bathed last, whether she'd been shuttered up here since she left my place. I wondered what she'd been doing to sustain herself. I nearly reached out again but held back; her breath was ragged, but her sobs had subsided, and she was not screaming anymore. Best for both of us to leave well enough alone.

I needed to think. I needed to figure out a next move. Or a first one. I felt like I had never figured out anything at all. If I could just get five minutes of silence. That didn't seem too much to ask. Being in this room felt like holding my breath; I could feel my lungs strain underneath my ribs. I glanced at Corrina once more — the rise and fall of her back the only movement — before I turned away. Through the door, I could see the living room, and the field of furniture in my way. The front door was closed, but I could almost smell the jasmine blooming in the night. It was so close, only a few steps, one after the other. After that, I'd be away from here. I reminded myself to close the doors behind me. No one needed to see this.

Then I turned back, once more, to be sure.

She wasn't by the bed any longer. I didn't see her anywhere. I stepped back into the room, scanning for her presence, feeling … not panic yet, but a rising tide of discomfort in my solar plexus. And then, for a while, I didn't feel anything at all.

People say they don't remember moments of great trauma. They say they go into a fugue state, or their fight-or-flight mechanism kicks in. I have no reason to doubt them, but that's not the way it was with me. I remember everything, the way her movements unfolded like a slide show, the jagged pulsing of a black-and-white film. Or no, not black-and-white, but a film that's jumped its sprockets, that flickers and skips and slides off-kilter, until the frame gets stuck in the gate and the image bubbles into flame. One moment, she was nowhere, and the next, she was rising before me like an enormous bird of prey. In the patchwork darkness, I could make out wings, or what looked like wings, although on the level of conscious reasoning, I knew they were bedsheets, wrapped around her like a second skin. Yet conscious reasoning — what was that? It seemed the rubric of a different world. In *this* world, I watched, feet stuck as if in mire, as she grew bigger, broader, filling up the room. The animal scent became overwhelming; it was as if I had been transported to a lion's den. Who had that been? Daniel? Joseph? Someone biblical. I didn't put much faith or credence in that book. Just a collection of tales, of stories, other than its assertion of a vengeful god. And where was I now except in such a presence, if not of God than perhaps its messenger? Angel or demon, what did it matter? I'd long understood there was no difference between the two. This was what I'd always known would be the outcome. This was recompense for everything I'd done. As she moved on me, I stood there undefended. It was what I had deserved all along.

If I said it seemed almost as if we were embracing, no one would believe me. But that's the way it was at first. Her fists, her fingernails, her teeth — all that came later, although later, what did that even mean in a room where time had stopped? I had the sense that I would never escape her, or that the world would be different if I did. Primordial, maybe, prehistoric, as if in entering her apartment I'd passed through a wormhole, a portal from which there was no way back. Under her mass, or the mass of those tangled bedsheets, I began to grow breathless, from the scent, the primal reek of her, but also from her weight. She did not exactly push me down or maybe she did; either way, I found myself sprawled across the carpet with her sitting on my chest. The roughness of the weave pressed its tattoo into the flesh of my back. I focused on that, tried to use it as a way of staying present, but all I really wanted was to go to sleep. Once she had me on the floor, she began to claw at me, arms first and then the chest, and finally the face. She was moaning lightly but not in language, or at least not any language that I knew. It was as if she were singing a lullaby, or a worksong, something to keep the rhythm going, to hold us both in place. When she raked my cheek for the first time, I flinched and thought about the blood. Then she raked me again, nails sharp and glistening now with a narrow trace of red that appeared to take shape in the darkness, as if it were something between us, another intimacy we had shared.

It could have gone on all night like this. Or maybe I was just trying to tire her out, although that seems too intentional. I could have thrown her off; if she was strong, I was stronger, but I didn't want to cause her pain. Better just to pay the price, to let her take this from me, and hope that afterward, she — both of us — might feel redeemed.

Then her voice began to rise again, and the wordless song that she'd been singing took shape in a different way. The syllables tightened, sharpened, reconfigured once again around the letters of my name.

"Corrina," I said. My voice rasped as if I'd never learned to speak.

"Don't you dare," she hissed. It could have been a trick of the light but I thought I saw her eyes flash, and then her hands began to tighten around my throat.

"Corrina," I said again, in a whisper. I drew a ragged breath through my nose.

"I told you," she answered, and her voice rose in one long ululating rhythm, and with that, the woman next door was screaming again. I imagined what might be happening in the courtyard, all the people in those other units opening their windows and standing close. They had heard her before but not like this. She kept pressing on my throat, and screaming.

I wanted the screaming to end.

You could say things got out of hand at that point, although that's not how I remember it, and I remember everything. More like there was one logical path to go down, one choice to make this go away. For so much of my life I'd been passive. I'd hung back in my marriage — as I'd hung back tonight. Now I was in the middle of existence and I was about to make my mark. Not the mark I would have wanted, not the mark I would have imagined, even a few minutes ago. But this was where I was. My options had boiled down to one. When she moved her hand from my throat to hit me again, I took my opportunity, thrusting upward with my chest and hips and catching her off balance, rolling over until I was now on top.

As for what happened next, I remember that also: the scuffle, her kicking and screaming, my hand over her mouth to muffle her. She bit my palm, and then again, tearing at the flesh there, but I had to make her stop. Eventually I covered her nose as well and then I pressed, as if to still the noise. She grew very quiet then, struggling until her struggling subsided, and she lay still amid the tangle on the floor.

When it was over, I went to the kitchen, ran the water hot and cold. I grabbed a clutch of paper towels and tried to clean my hands and face. *Out, out, damn spot*: it was hard without a mirror, but I didn't want to see myself. The air in the apartment had gone static, yielding to a suspended state. What if I had never been here? What if neither of us were? My blood, my fingerprints, were all over the place, but that wasn't such a problem; we had known each other, after all. Now, I needed a plan. I dried my hands and glanced at my phone: 1:30 a.m. It would be getting light in about four hours. I walked back to the bedroom, shut the door without looking inside. In the darkness and the silence, I took a deep and rectifying breath.

"What now?" I said aloud in the empty living

room. No answer was forthcoming, not that I'd expected one. The universe was a battlefield, it would destroy all of us in the end. Wasn't that what had just happened, another step on the passage to perdition, another irredeemable sin?

Not that I was sorry. I'd just needed her to stop.

Her purse, I saw now, was on the kitchen counter, that same small backpack, along with two grocery sacks. I opened it and began to root around. Everything was as it had been: the compact, the lipstick, and the wallet, which contained five new hundred dollar bills. I pocketed the money, put the wallet back inside. At the bottom of the bag, a hard plastic rectangle turned out to be the Prius key. I appropriated that also as an idea began to take shape in my head. Her car, I felt sure, was where it always was, by the entrance to the court. It was a quick and easy walk. At this hour, I could make it without notice, if I had a little luck. Absently, I reached back into the purse, closed my fingers around another shape. It was the thumb drive, the thumb drive I had put there. Such a small item, so inconsequential, although couldn't that be said of everything? We never knew what was going to take us down, what minor mistake or indecision might lead to the unraveling of the world. I couldn't even say why I had taken it, and yet now here we were. Nothing ever turned out as expected. Nothing ever went as it should.

I put the thumb drive in my pocket with the money and the keys.

QUESTION NUMBER SEVEN: SHOULD I PICK YOU UP AT QUARTER TO ELEVEN?

Here's a hard truth: guilt does not adhere. You do what you do and then you find a way to live with it. Or you don't, and it drives you mad. The key was not to forget about it — how could you forget about it, something that got at the very essence of your heart, the stain of your living? — but rather not to think about it. Not denial so much as a kind of conscious shutting down. You had to slow things, take each action step-by-step, concentrate only on what was in front of you, stop thinking and be where you were. This moment, and then this one, and then this one. Each with its own obligations and responsibilities. Such as: the obligation to get out of here without being noticed. The responsibility to cover your tracks. Time, that neverending torrent, carrying us all ceaselessly to the grave. It wasn't the grave that worried me, it was oblivion. And yet, I guess you could say I had found my own oblivion here on earth. In this bungalow court in Hollywood, I had come face-to-face with something I hadn't wanted to recognize or remember. Now I was living once more in the aftermath. But what was the alternative? What else was there for me to do? Nothing but to wait it out.

It's amazing how time, even just a bit of it, can assuage so much.

And time it was and what a time it was, and I was back in time once more. I could feel the relentless pull of it, the insistence that would not go away. It was late but also early. I had time but not a lot. Like the grocery sacks in Corrina's kitchen, the relics of a different time. Absently, I rifled through them. One was empty; the other held a box of safety matches, a can of lighter fluid, and a small bag of briquettes. My throat caught then and I faltered at the sad sweetness, the resignation and the hope. The small dreams were the ones that got me, the ones that could belong to anyone. It was such a minor aspiration: to behave, just once, as if you were a normal person, however you defined the term. To imagine you might invite some people over for a barbecue, sit out front on a summer evening and drink a few beers while flipping burgers on the grill. The shovel in my closet was like that also, a promise I had broken to myself. What did it say about us that we found it so difficult to function? What did it say that we couldn't do the simplest things?

Maybe that was why we'd been pulled into one another's orbits. Maybe that was why we'd washed up here.

The shovel. I was going to need that. I was going to put it to use. First, I had to take care of a few things, though, beginning with her purse. I put it in the empty grocery bag, rolled and bunched the top to make a seal. Outside, I tossed it in the dumpster. Not ideal, but it would have to do. At my place, I left the five hundred dollars in the dresser and grabbed the shovel, before going out to check the car. It was, as I'd imagined, parked on Franklin. I put the shovel in the empty trunk and went back to Corrina's, staying to the margins of the path. Then, I headed for the bedroom, to begin the dance of getting Corrina out the door. First I stood her up, my arm around her waist and hers over my shoulder so that if anyone were to see us, it would look, I hoped, like she was drunk. The lights were still out in the court, but that didn't mean anything; how many times had I watched from inside my dark apartment as she screamed into the night? In any case, it didn't matter. I didn't have a choice. I was in time now, and there was nothing else to do.

I wrestled Corrina to the front door and together, we stepped out into the night. She was heavier than I'd imagined, or more unwieldy; I almost dropped her going down the steps. I didn't think about the fact that she was dead — I focused on the chore. She had become cargo, a job, a task to be completed. She was no longer a human being. It was amazing how fast life could leave us. It was amazing how fast we could become slabs of meat. Living was hard, but dying was easy. She was out of her misery now, but me … I was walking into mine.

It took a few minutes to bring her to the sidewalk. I held my breath — at least it felt that way— the entire time. *Don't notice me, don't notice me*: prayer or mantra, wish fulfillment, the words beat a staccato pattern in my head. All my senses were heightened. It was as if I could see and hear everything. Not just here but across the city. If I concentrated hard enough, my vision could penetrate the walls.

And then, in the middle of it all, I knew that nothing would happen. I knew that I'd remain untouched. That was my punishment, to get away with it, to live with the knowledge of everything I'd caused. No one cared, it was like Kitty Genovese. If anything, they'd feel relief. Relief for the silence, relief that the screaming had stopped. And me? I was invisible, an exterminating angel. The path ahead was clear.

At the car, I slumped her into the passenger seat and shut the door. Just for the moment, just until I was away from here. I tried not to look as I came around to the driver's side and pulled out from the curb. A few blocks south, a small, abbreviated street dead-ended against the 101, and in the shadows of the freeway, I parked and transferred Corrina to the trunk. Once she was stowed, I got back behind the wheel and found the on-ramp, driving through the awful darkness towards the light I knew was coming, the light that would clarify and condemn me at once.

For a while, I drove without intention. I had an idea of where I was headed, but I didn't want to go there yet. Strange as it may sound, I felt free in the car. As long as I was driving, nothing had really happened yet. The freeways were empty, ribbons of cracked asphalt stretching into the darkness, glistening gray like rivers of little fish. I was one of those fish now, caught up in the current, window open, cool breeze of the after-midnight, and the smell of oil drifting up like vapor from the surface of the road. It had been so long since I'd gone on a night drive, since I'd been in a car in the smallest hours, alone in nearly every sense of the word. The last times had been when I was married — or more accurately, when the marriage was falling apart. Back then, I'd often lie in bed until my wife was sleeping before getting up, silent as a killer in the night. I'd slip on pants and shirt and shoes, pass noiselessly across the carpet to the front door, text her when I got outside. *Driving. Back by 8*, and then I'd shut off my phone and get in the car. The car, yes, the car that I had lost when the marriage ended, the car I didn't need anymore. By then, I'd discovered drinking — or not discovered but given myself over to it. Why leave when you could absent yourself from memory and from body, when you could do away with the torment of your dreams? In the before time, before I lost my wife, I didn't yet understand that consolation could be a commodity, something to be bought and sold. I'd head out on the 10 past Pomona, maybe get off in Claremont or Fontana and drive the local roads. South of the freeway, the Southern Pacific tracks stretched across the landscape like the ruins of some failed civilization. I loved the trains, sometimes I'd drive out here in the daytime just to see them, see the flatcars and the boxcars, all that commerce, all that rolling stock. It was possible, almost, in their presence to believe in something: some sort of order, or at least power, some sort of certainty and form. Trains had been rolling out here for a century and a half; they were a constant built across an inconstant landscape, oblivious to its fires and its floods. In the after hours, though, the tracks were just a smudge, a whisper, a breath in the empty darkness, something half-forgotten from a nightmare or a dream.

Forgetting, of course, was the point of living in Los Angeles. Everyone said so. I, however, saw it differently. For me, it was not forgetting, but rather distance: a means, a mechanism, to get away. I remembered everything about those drives I'd taken, just as I would remember everything about this one, especially its breadth and speed. Once I finally turned back west, I passed from downtown to Santa Monica in eleven minutes, the Prius the only car on either side of the road. I pushed the speed to eighty, then to ninety — a stupid move but one I felt helpless to resist. What if I got pulled over? I couldn't even say where the registration was, let alone my license, which in any case had lapsed. And then there was ... well, better not to say it. Better not to acknowledge what I knew. I felt the weight of circumstance, then, as it settled around my shoulders with the discomforting insistence of a shroud.

I followed the 10 through the McClure Tunnel and headed north on PCH. A few miles up, I got to Malibu, and turned off on one of the canyon roads. I'd been here before, but not for a long time, and I couldn't say what might have changed. I felt pieces of my former self come streaming back, like loose leaves caught in a breeze. The air was thick with salt, the greasy smell of the Pacific, which lapped at the lip of the land as hungrily as a predator's tongue.

Up here, it was inky dark, and a two-lane blacktop that coiled and curled. I wound my way into the hills, noticing the faint gray shapes of houses set back from the road. It was three in the morning and no one appeared to be awake. A curve, and then another, and now I was in the emptiness of the Southern California outback, adrift amid the stars as if I were the last person left alive on earth. I brought the car to a stop at a scenic overlook, not an official one but a ridge of flattened dirt along the edge of the tarmac. We had come here once, my wife and I, to this corner of the county that looked the same, I liked to imagine, as it had in the days of the Tongva, before the city had been built. Southern California was full of these little patches of wildness, places where if you squinted in the right way, the last four hundred years of history might seem to erase itself. This was what I wanted — erasure, disappearance, not of myself but of the world. I wanted to live in a blank landscape, with no attachments, no connections, no other people, nothing but myself. Solipsism, you might call it, although, as I had come to learn, solipsism is more complicated than it appears. My brand was what the philosophers called *metaphysical*. But what did I know of philosophy? To me, it only confirmed what I already knew.

The problem was that knowledge didn't change anything. What you knew could be a delusion or a lie. What you knew could put you at risk. Take this situation. Soon, the night would bleed out at its edges into early morning, and the horizon would bruise from black to purple, a purple that would lighten towards rose. Now that I was here, I wanted time to stop again, but there was only one way for that to occur. One way? Not even. Like the living, the dead were still constrained by time. Corrina … she might not know it any longer, but she was here, an impediment to be dealt with, a roadblock in the middle of my life. I could have just left her in the apartment, but how could I? I didn't want her to be found.

Time would never leave any of us alone.

I opened the trunk and withdrew the shovel, averting my eyes from the other cargo there. In the dark, this was easier than expected, almost as if I had imagined it all. I shut the trunk again and locked it, slid down the backside of the hill beneath the ridge. Wild rye, coyote bush, purple sage, and yarrow: the brush was tenacious. I felt its nettles tug at my pants, my ankles, like hands determined to pull me down.

At the bottom of the slope was a clearing, a copse of willow and chaparral. My wife and I had visited at the finish of our marriage, a desolate and dangerous time. We had done damage to ourselves, we understood that, although neither of us wanted to make repairs. We'd veer from silence to wild abandon, committing extreme and risky acts. This had been the latter, heightened by the car we'd left on the turnout above. That was part of the thrill, wasn't it? That someone, maybe the police, might think we were in distress and come looking, that someone might stumble across us and we'd be found out. Now, I was here again, in a similar circumstance, hoping the darkness would cover me. What would I say if an officer appeared, at the top of the ridge, looking for the driver of the Prius, flashlight cutting through the darkness like a blade? There would be nowhere to hide, nowhere to turn, no excuse or logic I could name. The thought of it sent a sharp, wincing jolt through my intestines and tightened my sphincter. I took a breath and got to work.

At the edge of the copse, I dug out a shallow oblong, not a grave so much as a gesture of concealment, a place for her to hide. The earth was rocky and recalcitrant, and it took all I had to carve the shape of it, make it long enough, and wide. I cut down into the earth as deeply as I could, but I didn't have the necessary strength, and the shovel had not been made for this. And yet, time kept moving; I could see it in the sky. Just since I'd arrived, the night had begun to soften and grow dusky with the promise of emerging light. I didn't want to think about that. I didn't want to know the hour. That jolt in my guts, the fire of it, came back, a rush of ... not fear but something like it. I swallowed back its searing agony.

And then it was finished, or finished enough. It was time to take care of the final part. I crawled up the hill to bring her down. She was waiting for me, and as I lifted her, I flashed back to the night of my wedding, the two of us, my wife and I, a little drunk, a little giddy, when I carried her across the threshold of our hotel room. The evening had been a lot like this one, cool coming on the heels of bitter heat. We'd watched the firmament lighten throughout that long night also, shifting in increments from plum to lavender to gold as the sun peeked over the horizon before rising like a beacon in the sky. I remembered I had almost dropped her; it was awkward to carry another human being. We had giggled as I wrestled with the door.

Well, that was a long time ago. Another lifetime, another world. Tonight, I wasn't giggling, I was struggling, hefting Corrina as if she were a bag of coal. The easiest thing was to hoist her over my shoulder. That way, I didn't have to see the curve of her chin, the blue streaks in her hair, her eyes open and staring out of the maw of their own emptiness. The brush had other ideas, though

— again, it pulled. A few yards below the turnout, I lost my balance, and as I stumbled, I gave up my grip. Corrina tumbled down the hillside, body cutting a loose trail through the wild growth. I half-slid behind her, not even trying to catch myself.

At the bottom, I hefted her once more and hauled her to the space that I had dug. Then I fitted her inside. The hole was broad enough but far too shallow, I could see that even as I began to shovel back the dirt. She kept looking at me with those eyes, their flecks of lavender, less pleading than ... acknowledging. The sky was filtering to gray now, and I was exposed, in the open, working with the shovel as if by rote. Nothing left to do but finish — although even after I'd smoothed and spread the dirt, the earth offered only the thinnest of veneers. It was just a matter of time before wind or rain revealed her, or an animal caught her scent and dug her up. I had left tracks, and they would be discovered, would lead whoever was looking all the way back down the PCH and on the freeway out across the basin to the bungalow court. Some exterminating angel. How had I thought I would not be found out? I felt panic then, felt it rise within me, like a cold finger at the back of my throat.

For a minute, I paced a ragged circle in the clearing. Nothing to do but leave it to chance. I climbed back up the hill to the Prius, opened the trunk to put the shovel back. And that was when I saw it: the second grocery sack. How had it gotten here? Inside, I could make out the lighter fluid and the matches, the bag of briquettes. I was trying to remember, I had used the empty one to hide her purse, but this? I'd left it on the kitchen counter, I knew I had. That cold finger in my throat grew thicker, became the suffocating pressure of her hands on my neck.

And yet, here it was, the answer, to a question I hadn't known to ask. It didn't matter how it had happened. It only mattered that it had. Call it a blackout or a benediction. Call it a miracle or a myth. Whatever way I chose to frame it, this was a gift from the capricious universe. I shook the can of lighter fluid. Twelve ounces, according to the label — and it was full. I returned it to the sack with the briquettes and the matches, and carried everything back down the hill.

In the gathering grayness, the copse was silent as a churchyard. If I held my breath, I could almost imagine the presence of a shape or spirit, not God but some other essence, a monster from a different time. I'd read about the tahquitz and the chupacabras — but this didn't feel like that. More like the Dark Watchers, those phantoms who emerge at twilight in the Santa Lucia Mountains near Monterey. Monterey wasn't Malibu, and twilight wasn't daybreak, but maybe they were close enough, in an inverted sort of way. Certainly, there were monsters in these hills, and the remains of those who'd crossed their paths. You might say this was what had happened to Corrina, although I preferred not to think of it that way.

I kept my eyes to the ground as I returned to her, gathering loose brush and kindling. I piled them on the mound of dirt that marked her place. Then I went back for larger branches, and layered them on top. When I was finished, I sprinkled the briquettes and sprayed lighter fluid across the length and breadth of it, until I'd emptied the can. My eyes watered at the scent, the pungent distillation of the naphtha and the kerosene. Next, I opened the box of matches, withdrew the first thin filament of wood. I couldn't shake the feeling that this had been intended: the way the pieces had all fallen into place. Predestination, you might call it, except I didn't know what that meant. You had to make your own luck, to fight your own way through the world. I lit a match, dropped it on the briquettes and branches; it flitted out before anything could spark. The second match was more effective, and the third and the fourth — nice and easy, nothing too dramatic, and then those first few shoots of flame were lapping at the kindling, the way the ocean had lapped against the shore.

It was time to leave now, time to say goodbye. But first, I needed to make sure. I sprinkled the rest of the matches over the growing conflagration; they sparked in little bursts of phosphorous. I stood there for another minute, watching as the flames began to erase Corrina from this world. It was as if, having completed its forward movement, time had begun moving backwards, and I would arrive at home to find that none of this had ever taken place. Wishful thinking again, of course it was. But in that moment, I imagined it might lead me to a state of grace. The dawn was rising, the sky lightening with the haste of day emerging, like an animal roused from sleep. In the quiet of the canyon, I could hear the rustle of the wind through the eucalyptus and the sycamore. The fire continued rising; I could feel its heat now, and smell not just the lighter fluid but also the burning wood. In the chill of the encroaching morning, I reached out to warm my hands. Then I turned and went back up the hill to return to the city, but not before I reached into my pocket and withdrew the thumb drive, which I tossed into the center of the pyre.

I found a space on one of the small streets south of Franklin, in the amorphous territory between the flats of Hollywood and the hills. This was the Los Angeles where I felt comfortable, neither one thing nor the other, neither here nor there. Eventually, the Prius would be towed or ticketed, but that was not my problem. I opened the glove box and removed the registration, shuffled through the papers there for anything that could connect the car to her. I thought about removing the license plates, but that seemed too suspicious; I didn't want to draw attention to myself. Then I caught a glimpse of my face in the rearview and saw the lacerations, and I remembered it was much too late for that.

I popped the trunk and grabbed the shovel and the grocery sack, which held the empty briquette bag and lighter fluid can. I stuffed the registration in my pocket. It felt like I was forgetting something, but I couldn't say what that might be. It was a little after six a.m., and to the north and west, the horizon was pale blue behind a layer of morning mist. Here, the air felt thick and close and difficult to breathe.

I locked the car and walked away.

At this early hour of the morning, everyone in Hollywood looked as bad as I did. That was the good news. The tourist locations weren't open; the unhoused slept in doorways, or in tents erected under freeway overpasses, their belongings bundled tight around the spaces where they lay. On Yucca, I dropped the shovel in a trash can, and left the grocery bag in another one a few blocks away. I tore up Corrina's registration, released the shredded paper to the air. A light breeze swirled the scraps briefly around my head as if they were a cloud of ash.

I kept to the side streets; it seemed the safest way. Whitley, Cherokee, Las Palmas — the dingbats and apartment complexes, the crumbling craftsmen, everything coated with dust and grime. People don't think about Hollywood as a place; they imagine it as a label. They talk about it as if it's magical, but for me, it's just the opposite, a sprawling neighborhood that reveals itself in the sagging shoulders of its frame houses, all those yards fenced off with chain link. It's not that it's tired, exactly, although resignation does live on these streets. But so do families, working people, janitors and car mechanics and cleaning women, kids skateboarding after school. There's nothing fancy here, nothing but desire and aspiration and frustration, too little money and not enough time. Just the way it is for everyone in the purgatory of the city, another world from all those mansions on the hill.

And me, I was deep inside that purgatory. Who was I kidding? I had always been. Hollywood was a place to get lost. And getting lost, it turned out, suited me. Being seen was the last thing I wanted, especially on a morning such as this one, my clothing tinged with the reek of lighter fluid and those scratches on my face.

Then, just a few blocks from the bungalow court, the stillness was disrupted by a blur of motion, and the walker turned into my path. He was wearing his brown UCLA sweatshirt, and as usual, he seemed preoccupied, lost inside his head. His hair was wild, and his eyes were blazing, and his gaze seared my skin. As I approached, he appeared to glare at me. Then he began to speak.

"I left it for you," he said, voice thick and throaty. "I left it for you to find."

What? I wanted to ask. *What are you talking about, old man?* But it was as if a spell had been broken, as if now that he had spoken, there was nothing else to say. I waited for a moment, feeling invisible no longer. He stared as I crossed the street.

I forced myself not to look back at him.

At my place, everything was quiet. I could see a few lights, and hear the low murmur of news drifting from an open window, but the morning felt if not quite safe than something close to calm. I took a deep breath. My apartment was less than forty feet away. Forty feet and I'd be free. I wanted to run, but I kept my pace. No reason to rush things now.

Inside, I locked the door and lowered the shades. Then, I poured a drink. As I sipped, I could feel my tension begin to loosen, the heat rising in my limbs. I finished my drink and poured another. What did I care that it was not yet seven? I'd had a long night, and I'd been working, and now I was seeking out a place of shelter from a storm I hadn't known was coming until it had arrived. What had I imagined was going to happen? It was a question I didn't know how to answer. I wanted to withdraw, to hide out until I was forgotten, and with me, everything I'd ever done.

I poured a third drink and switched on the receiver, turning the volume as low as it could go and still be heard. Through the speakers, I could make out the tinny treble of an acoustic guitar, and then the high fine tenor of Bukka White rising like a plaint or a lament. "Parchman Farm Blues," recorded in Chicago in 1940, after he'd spent three years in the Mississippi state prison — the infamous Parchman — for killing someone, he insisted, in self-defense. Well, I had acted in self-defense also. What other choice had I had? She had attacked me. I had the scratches to prove it, wasn't that the case? I took out my phone and shot a selfie, and another, before enlarging both images, my face distorting as it grew. The blood had dried, but now the scabbing cut my cheeks into a jagged matrix of angry lines.

I thought about getting cleaned up, but who was going to see me now? The walker was still out there, wandering the streets like a Dark Watcher, but he wasn't anything to me. In the city of night, I had worried about being caught, but I had moved across the landscape as unseen as an angel or a ghost. As if I were a Dark Watcher myself, materializing in the seam between the day and the night. Maybe that was what he'd left me. Maybe that was why he'd glared. In any case, whatever I was or might have been, it had felt real out there, as if something were at stake. Now, I wanted to wear the stain of it. I wanted to bear the mark.

For so long, my life had been about trying to feel nothing. My life had been about trying to stay numb. Whatever else might have happened, I no longer felt that way. Instead, it was as if I'd been … unleashed, as if there were an animal stirring inside my soul. I felt sanctified in violence, and in rage. I thought about the man who'd been arrested for those car fires, the one everybody said they couldn't understand. He'd been driven by loss, they'd said, of course they did, but I knew it was different — that those fires had been lit out of wrath and retribution, out of the need, or the desire, to strike back. Briefly, I remembered the fire I had just set before I pushed it from my mind. I would know, we would all know, how it played out soon enough. In the meantime, all I wanted was to sit here in the slipstream, in a morning that was not a morning, in a morning that still felt like night. *See you in church*, a bartender I'd once known had liked to say on Saturdays when he was closing. The idea was that you needed to sin so you'd have something to pray about or to repent. I didn't know about that; every prayer I'd ever uttered had gone unanswered.

That was why I didn't pray.

I poured a last drink — just one more, I told myself — tapping my foot to Bukka White as he sang about how the judge had given him life this morning, down on Parchman Farm.

QUESTION NUMBER EIGHT:
IS IT A DATE?

I slipped out of time there, for a little while. Run to ground, run like the hunted, even though no one, it seemed, was looking for me. I slept most of the first day, waking to use the bathroom, and once or twice to eat. The sleep was restless, a series of small tempests more hallucinated than dreamed. I kept losing myself, my sense of place, of person; I kept losing my grip on who and where I was. In the darkness, it was as if I were entombed. No light, no stimulus — a cocoon, I suppose, although I was past the point of metamorphosis. Reverse metamorphosis was more like it, as if I had turned into a giant bug. Once, in the bathroom, I caught a glimpse of my face in the mirror and I almost couldn't recognize it: a few days of stubble and those long red angry scratches, evidence of where I'd been. The further I got from it, the more it too felt like a dream or a hallucination, something that couldn't have happened, which was the same as saying that it never did.

When the knocking started, it sounded as if it were coming from underwater, like the noise a boat makes in a storm. Boom, and then again, low along the hull line: Boom. I was in bed, underneath a thin sheet, skin dampened with sweat. It was hot but I didn't want relief from it. I didn't want any comfort at all.

I let the knocking go on for what felt like a few minutes. The darkness occluded everything. My palms began to tingle, and a buzzing rose up in the back of my skull. What day was it? Who could say anymore? Was it possible I could have been found out? In the end, I had been careful, I was sure of that. No one but the walker had noticed as I made my way home. I had drifted through the dawning streets as translucent as a glimmer, a twist of smoke in (slightly) human form.

My first thought was to ignore it, but that seemed

unwise. If it was the police, they would come through the door one way or another. Hesitating would only bring attention I did not want or need. The key was to maintain a low profile, to stay unnoticed, the shade or shadow I wished to be. The key was to keep myself inviolable, to float above until it had ceased to matter, until it was no longer a concern. My head was foggy, but that was nothing unfamiliar. I got up and inched my way out of the bedroom, the carpet rough and caustic underneath my feet.

In the living room, I could see a pale scrim at the edges of the curtains: a ghost of light, only a rumor, a whisper, piercing the faded border of the day. That meant it was either early morning or early evening. Both, I realized, were the same to me. I had withdrawn from time, just the way I'd always wanted. I had removed myself from the tumult of the world. But that was just a fantasy, wasn't it? For here was the world again, thrusting itself back on me as ever, banging on my door.

I wasn't expecting to see Sylvia, or maybe I'd forgotten her, left her in the clearing with Corrina, left her in the past. But there she was, on the stoop when I opened the door. I flinched as if she might attack me; I cringed like an animal afraid of being hit. I ducked my head and backed away, and in that moment, I gave up my power, although I'd never had any power with her anyway. Sylvia watched me, and her lips curved into a tight grin. It was not mirth but malice that I saw reflected, as if some hidden something, some kind of secret, had only just now been confirmed.

"Get in a fight?" she asked, no preamble, gesturing at my face.

"Cut myself shaving," I said.

She laughed, a short sharp burst that crackled like a flame.

Then she stepped around me and into the living room. As she passed, I caught a whiff of her perfume. It smelled like money, as if the essence of some privilege, some assurance had been distilled. I stood there waiting for it to dissipate. I did not want to go inside. In the empty space where she'd been standing, the sky was amber. Behind the perfume, I could make out the sharper scent of smoke.

Inside, Sylvia glanced around as if disgusted. The air was stale, and a layer of dust lingered on nearly every surface. I went to shut the bedroom door; when I returned, she had taken a seat — gingerly, as if not wishing to be soiled — on the lip of the couch. I had a flashback to the first night Corrina had come here; she'd sat in the same spot. Sat? Sprawled out drunken, legs akimbo, as if the place belonged to her. I remembered having to clean the bathroom and how everything had happened after that. If only I hadn't opened the door. If only I had let her scream. It had been quiet these last few nights (how many?) but that was deceptive. It didn't include the noise inside my head. And now, here I was, having opened the door again. Here I was with another wild card in the room.

Sylvia, however, was a portrait of self-containment. She remained silent for so long that I began to wonder if she would acknowledge me again. It was a waiting game, but I was sick of waiting. I wanted the waiting to be done. I wanted to be away from these people, like characters in a story I no longer wanted to tell. I stood up, made my way into the kitchen, and returned with a fresh bottle of Maker's and two glasses.

"Drink?" I asked, my voice as dry as the still air.

"It's seven thirty in the morning," she said. "Are you sure you want to start your day like that?"

Seven thirty in the morning? Well, if nothing else, that settled the question of dusk or dawn. Now that I knew, I could feel time start to move again. Whatever sanctity or distance I might have carved out began to dissipate.

"Go ahead if you want," she continued. "You look like you could use it." She laughed again, a bitter bark. "I can't imagine where you've been."

"I …" I sputtered, but she cut me off:

"I don't want to know."

I didn't want her to notice my weakness. I wanted

to be strong and resolute. As always, though, I was un-settled by her presence, the way she excited and repelled me at once. This morning, she was in a tailored skirt and blouse with matching sweater, thin gold chain around her neck. She sat with her hands folded, but I could see clear polish on her fingers, the elegance of her manicure. I stud-ied the line of her chin and felt myself drifting. She looked like my wife, if my wife had been older. I poured myself a splash of Maker's and sat down.

"I've come," Sylvia said, "to find out what you knew about Corrina. She seems to have ... disappeared."

"Disappeared?" I repeated, voice thick.

"She's not at home and her car is missing. What other word would you use?"

Sylvia looked up, her eyes like lasers sparking red. I could feel them piercing, feel their tendrils reach in-side me, rewiring my circuits as if they now belonged to her. It was as if I didn't need to say anything. It was as if she already knew. I felt helpless, unable to protect my secrets. It was as if she could see everything.

"I haven't seen her," I replied.

"How long since you and she were last in touch?"

"I don't know. Maybe a week? It's not like I've been keeping track."

"I understand that there was screaming. A few nights ago."

"There was screaming most nights, Sylvia. You know that."

She stared at me again, those gray eyes flinty. "Yes," she said. "I guess I do."

"Look, Sylvia. Why do you care? If she's gone, doesn't that make it easier for you?"

"You would think so, wouldn't you? But it com-plicates the legal issues. Unless her disappearance is re-solved."

"Resolved?" I couldn't hear what she was saying. Wasn't the fact that she was gone enough? Without mean-ing to do so, I had cleared a path for her. And maybe, I began to think, also for myself.

And then it dawned on me what she had meant.

"You need her to be dead …" I whispered.

I did not want to say another word.

"Well," she answered, and laughed once more, throatier this time. The smell of her perfume mingled with the tart bite of the whiskey. Briefly, I imagined putting on some music, just to break the ice. But the ice had been broken that first afternoon in Benedict Canyon. There had never been anything between us except for this.

"I don't expect anything from you," she went on. "I just need to know that she's not coming back."

"I'm sorry," I said.

"I can make it worth your while."

She withdrew a sealed business envelope and set it lightly on the table. In the dimness of the morning, it glowed translucent white.

"Your face suggests you might know more than you are saying."

I didn't trust her but I couldn't help myself.

"She may," I murmured, "have said something about Malibu."

"Malibu's on fire."

"What?" I felt a web of doubt begin to settle around me, as if I had been swept up in a net.

"Wildfire. Up in the canyons. Started a couple of days ago."

"Shit," I answered, and in that moment, I couldn't have said if I was referring to the situation or acknowledging my guilt.

Sylvia looked at me, eyebrows curving into a pair of sidelong question marks. Anxiety began to work its way into my heart. *Don't say a word*, I told myself. *Don't look away*. But the more I kept my eyes on hers, the more I felt like prey.

"I don't think she's coming back," I said at last. It was a way to change the subject without changing the subject. I needed to get her out of here so I could find out what I'd done. I finished my drink and poured another. I didn't care what she might think. The room felt hot, although it had been hot already. I had been in this sort of situation before. What it required was a steadiness I was having difficulty mustering. I couldn't let her see the cracks.

Sylvia picked up the unused glass from the table and went to the kitchen. I could hear the faucet running in the sink. When she returned, it was as if something had been decided. She did not sit down as she spoke.

"I need to be sure," she said. "I need evidence."

The word rang like an alarm between us. I thought about what I might have left behind. Was it possible that we created traps for ourselves? Was it possible that we laid the groundwork for our fates? Certainly, that seemed true of Corrina, each poor decision or bit of bad luck leading to another until she had nowhere to turn. Could it be that she'd been complicit in all of them? But fate was a lie, wasn't it? The universe didn't care what happened to us. For proof, all I had to do was look at where I was right now, drinking in the dirty morning light with Sylvia in my living room. Although it was also the case that my bad choices had brought me here.

"You know," Sylvia said, "she was in rehab more than once. The first place was in Malibu." There was a musing aspect to her voice. "She insisted. I thought it was a bad idea. Who goes to rehab in Malibu? One night, she just walked out of the facility and called a cab to bring her home."

"Rehab?"

"Don't be stupid. You know she was a mess."

I couldn't help but notice she was using the past tense.

"That was the first 5150. There was no other choice. She was into everything: drugs, alcohol, food, sex addiction. Eventually, she agreed to go to a different facility in Arizona. Middle of nowhere. Impossible to escape. After her ninety days was up, she went into sober living. Then we moved her here." Sylvia took a sip of water. "Or my husband did. I told him he should cut her off."

"I've been in her apartment," I muttered numbly.

"Then you know what she did with my husband's

money. One of the first things I want to do is get rid of all that furniture so the place can be leased out."

"What if she comes back?"

"That's not my problem. In any case, I don't suspect she will."

"But you don't know for sure."

"No," she said, and her lips curled into a vicious smile. It was a fearsome thing to see. "But I imagine you can help with that. I imagine you know all sorts of things."

After she left, I filled my glass again. I sat for a long time in my chair. The room remained charged with her presence, as if a part of her, her anima, had lingered. Did the scratches on my face give me away? Certainly, they were another kind of evidence, a confession written in crusted lines of red. Absently, I picked at one scab until it broke off, and I could feel the wetness of fresh blood.

The envelope was where she had left it. I reached over and slowly worked the seal. Inside, I could see the pale green glint of money, a thin sheaf of hundred dollar bills. There was Ben Franklin looking back at me, narrow lips pursed in disappointment or dismay. But what did he know? He'd been dead forever, just like everyone. What did it matter how and when? What did it matter how old he might have been? The meaning of life was that it stopped, and that was not a meaning I could use. I counted the money, slamming the bills down on the table as I did: one hundred, two hundred, three hundred, four. There were ten in all, a thousand dollars, a thousand dollars for my soul. This was all that I was worth to her. I felt rage bubble up inside me. Or maybe that was just release.

I swept an arm across the table. The Maker's shattered as it hit the floor. I picked up the bills and threw them, watched them flutter as they fell. It felt as if the tension of the last few days was exploding. My body felt like it might blow apart. Without thinking, I began to scream. Like Corrina, the lines between us obscured and blurring, as if it had been me screaming all along. I wailed into the void of my apartment, no longer caring whether anyone noticed or heard. What could they do to me that I had not done already? Why shouldn't they confront my untamed rage? A thousand dollars was what it came to. A thousand dollars was an expression of my worth. Maybe it was good to know how little I mattered. Maybe it was good to know exactly who I was. Maybe it was time to face it all. I cried out in my anger, and I cried out in my fear. When I was finished, I left the money and the broken bottle where they'd fallen and retreated to the bedroom, where I opened the computer to get a sense of how things stood.

The fire was everywhere, that was the main thing. It had swept out of the canyon and eaten through a chunk of Topanga State Park. Now it was moving on the city, fanned by a rising Santa Ana that was blowing the flames south and east. Homes in Brentwood and the Palisades had been evacuated, and Beverly Hills looked like it could be at risk. The 405 had been positioned as a firebreak, with crews staked out around the Getty and the Brentwood Country Mart. Santa Monica was also threatened, north of Montana — the nicer sections, where the wealthy lived.

My wife had liked it there. It was where she wanted to end up. She had wanted a compound, a place with grounds, maybe a guesthouse. She had wanted privacy, a high hedge. For her … predilections, yes, but also because it was supposed to stay between her and me. Yet that privacy had turned to secrecy, and those secrets, they had become what we kept from one another, rather than what we shared. It's not that I came clean after it was over. It's not that I ever said a word. I had wanted the secrets also, had wanted to withdraw. That was how I landed here, in this corner of the city. It was not a consequence, it was a choice. In the other units, there were different sorts of people, some on the way up and some on the way down. Me, I was in the middle, neither here nor there. Or at least, that's how it had been until Corrina came knocking. Now as I watched footage of the flames on my computer, I could see the scope of everything she'd caused. The idea of it was overwhelming, such a big event starting from one so small. It was as if the embers had been sparked that first evening, as if that was when the fire had begun. I clicked through a few news sites, looking for reports about the fire's origin, looking to see if anything had been found. No one had any information. Or if they did, they weren't sharing it publicly. Instead, it was the same chaos everywhere: zero containment, and the winds expected to be heavy for a few days. I'd lived here long enough to know what this meant: that the danger was far from done.

But here I was, safe — for the moment, anyway. Nobody had anything on me. Nobody but Sylvia, that is, which was another problem, or maybe it was not. I remembered the scent of her perfume. I remembered the gray of her glare. If I closed my eyes, I could almost summon the sharp line of her jaw. Then I remembered I didn't have to summon anything. It was all here, available to me. In the heat of everything, I'd forgotten about the website and the thumb drive. That drive was now committed to the fire, but I had never taken the images down. I clicked over to see if they were still there. Sure enough: the traffic had long since gone static, but the pictures remained searchable if you knew to look for them.

And this I could understand, it had a pattern I could see. Not like Sylvia with her cryptic riddles, her hints and insinuations. This was photographic evidence, down in black and white. I wondered what she'd say if she knew I had made these posts. Maybe it would make her go away. I wanted to get clear but there was something about her that wouldn't leave me alone. It was more than her beauty; in Southern California, beauty was as common as it got. No, what drew me to Sylvia was different — let's call it force of will. My wife had been possessed of a similar quality, and she had used it to coerce me into sublimating my desires for hers. Now she was gone, and Sylvia … well, Sylvia was another matter, dangerous in a different way. Sylvia would have no qualms about setting me up, just to watch me fall. I clicked the link and there she was. I scrolled through the images one by one, looking at them in a desultory way. There was something here that I was missing. Something that didn't quite make sense. Again, I wondered about the photographer. A friend? Someone they'd hired? How much did it pay? Surely, it would have been a cash deal; no one would want invoices or receipts.

Then, I recalled the thousand dollars, and my body flushed with shame.

I closed the computer and returned to the living room. It smelled like whiskey from the broken bottle on the floor. It was time to get clean, to sort a few things; it was time to get my life under control. I grabbed a wad of paper towels and picked up the shards of glass. Then I blotted the liquid and mopped the floor, sharp scent of ammonia in my nostrils like the residue of a drug. It didn't make me high exactly, just a little focused, like a rail of meth. The feeling came in a shooting rush, the jangly charge of it, as if I could get away with everything. I plumped the cushions on the sofa, where Sylvia had just been sitting, and did the same to my chair. I dusted the coffee table and the counters and washed the glasses we had used. I thought about taking out the trash, but it was midday, and I didn't want anyone to see my face. Instead, I drew back the curtains to let in the dirty light. When I opened the windows, though, the air that came in through the screens smelled of burning wood. For a moment, I just stood there, confronted by the weight of it. Then I shut the windows, and let the curtains fall back into place. The money was still where I had tossed it; as I bent to pick it up, bill by bill, I noticed the sequence: LA15240990C, LA15240991C, LA15240992C. She'd probably had her personal banker deliver them. But why not? That was Sylvia's world. It wasn't the amount that was the insult, it was that it was so meaningless to her. Not hush money, or even a payment for … what? Taking care of an important mission? But I was not her emissary. Corrina had paid me in hundreds also, in the same dismissive sort of manner. Then she had used it to coerce me, as if I were her property.

Maybe the two of them were more alike than they had known.

I set the hundreds in a loose stack and left them in the bedroom, on the bureau next to my keys. I was slick with perspiration, not the flop sweat of this morning, but the sheen of activity. Maybe I should take up running. Maybe I should get some exercise. But no, Los Angeles was burning and the air quality was hazardous. Better to wait for the flames to dissipate. In the meantime, I had a clean apartment. In the meantime, I had turned the corner on the past. I went into the kitchen and pulled a fresh bottle of Maker's from the cabinet. It may have been early, but my luck was changing. I splashed a generous belt into a glass and set the stereo to play. In spite of how it had started, this was shaping up to be a decent day.

Through the speakers, I could hear a fluid line of boogie-woogie piano — the opening licks of Big Joe Turner and Pete Johnson's "Roll 'Em Pete." The live version from the first From Spirituals to Swing concert, presented at Carnegie Hall in 1938. Everyone called "Rocket 88" the earliest rock 'n' roll song, but this was the real point of ignition: the head-shaking rhythm, the rolling, driving beat. I bounced loosely back and forth as I sipped my drink. People liked to think they knew things but it was just what they'd been told. Rock 'n' roll couldn't have existed in 1938 because it hadn't been invented. But where did they think it came from? Nothing was ever invented, it was all waiting to evolve or be discovered, waiting for someone to give it a name. Nothing ever changed or turned out different; we just went through the motions of imagining that it could. The only thing that mattered was the moment. There was no future and no past. Big Joe Turner and Pete Johnson had been dead for a long time. And yet, just listen to those fingers on that keyboard. Listen to the timbre of that voice. They sounded ancient because they were ancient. But they also sounded very much alive.

I got a gal, she lives up on the hill

Something similar might be said of me, I supposed, although Sylvia was hardly a gal, and it would be a stretch to say I had her — more the other way around. Still, I couldn't help but feel that the song was a message of a kind. Certainly, it seemed to be my story Turner was shouting back across the decades:

Well, you're so beautiful, you've got to die someday

The thought gave me a shudder, as if I had brushed up against a ghost. A ghost, yes, or maybe walked across my own grave, one of those superstitions we can't quite shake. We know better but we still believe them. We hold onto them like faith. I left the music playing as I went to put the hundred dollar bills away.

It wasn't like I needed the money. I hadn't even spent Corrina's cash. I had stashed it in a drawer. That's what I would do with these bills also. Then I would try to forget that they were there. I had become involved in this as a lark, but it had gotten out of hand. Now I was done. I dug through the dresser for Corrina's seven hundred dollars. I added the five hundred I had taken from her wallet, and collated the three sheaves into one. Twenty-two hundred dollars in crisp bills. An idea started to form, or maybe an escape plan, but I couldn't quite make out what it was. Twenty-two hundred wouldn't be enough to do much, but it might buy me a little time or leeway — if, that is, the shit came down.

I thumbed through the bills as if they were the pages of a flip book. But the image on each page appeared the same. The money was so clean I could almost forget the shit I'd done to get it, even though it didn't mean anything to me. No story here, no salvation, no satisfaction at the end. Until ... there it was, like a secret message: another unexpected piece of evidence.

Sylvia's bills had consecutive serial numbers. I'd already noticed that. But now I could see that Corrina's came from the same sequence, both the money she'd given me and that which I had taken, although from a little earlier in the thread. LA15240920C, LA15240921C — those were the first two. The second payment picked up with LA15240922C, and that last five hundred with LA15240927C. Clearly, there had been more contact than she or Sylvia had acknowledged. Clearly, there was more going on than I had understood. I thought back to my first conversation with Sylvia, when she'd told me that Corrina was spoiled. I had seen it also, but now, all of that was now up in the air. What did it mean that they had been in contact? What did it mean that they were spending money from the same set of bills? The questions made me uneasy. I flicked the bills against my open hand, and thought about my next move.

It looked like I'd be going back up on the hill.

QUESTION NUMBER NINE: WHERE TO DINE?

Benedict Canyon Drive was thick with traffic: cars and emergency vehicles. People leaned forward behind their windshields, eyes narrowed and mouths agape. Everything felt up in the air, suspended, as if this were the last moment before the panic settled in. The fire was still on the other side of the 405, but even through the closed windows of the Lyft I could smell it, and flakes of white ash fell in lazy flurries from the smudged and dirty sky. The air looked singed: brown and dusky. Through the haze, the sun burnt orange-red, like the head of a safety match at the instant the sulfur explodes into flame.

In the front, the driver was talking. "I don't know why everybody's so worked up. News says they're getting it contained."

Hearing him made me want to get out of the car and set this hill ablaze.

I nodded and kept silent. I didn't want him to hear my voice. I was wearing my blue suit, and the red tie I'd had to knot three times. It still hung a little long. I'd waited a few days, until the marks on my face faded from angry scarlet to a kind of newborn pink. They inched across my cheeks like nascent worms. I looked almost presentable for the first time since ... but what was the point in going there? I had decided to purge it from my mind. That meant the fire, yes, but also Corrina, who was beginning to feel once again as if she were a tulpa, a figure from a dream.

I remembered those car fires in my neighborhood, the greasy chemical stench of them, the fear. I thought about what had lingered — not the fires so much as their effect. The disorder they provoked had seemed important, but now it was less than nothing, no one remembered anymore. The same would be true of this fire also, and the next one.

The same would be true of everything.

An image began to flicker at the edge of my consciousness like a candle burning, a candle in the shape of a woman as she screamed. I could almost see her, almost hear her, until I pushed her back below the surface of my mind. It wouldn't do to be unguarded. It wouldn't do to be vulnerable or distracted when I arrived. As usual, I was showing up unannounced, without a plan of action. I wanted to believe that gave me the element of surprise.

The driver turned off Benedict Canyon and into Sylvia's driveway. He pulled up in front of the fountain and put the car in park. Outside, the smell of fire was overwhelming, and to the west the sky reflected orange with its glow. That was the thing about the hills. People lived here — if they could afford to — because it allowed them to imagine they had risen above the world. That was fine in good times, with views that stretched as far as the Pacific, or east to the San Gabriels, which glimmered, snow-capped and mirage-like, in the distance beyond downtown. You could pretend that you were at the peak, the center, and also keep yourself apart. In bad times, though, everything was different, and being up here felt like living under siege. You could see the danger coming, but where was there to run? Those drivers on Benedict Canyon were discovering this now. Two lanes of blacktop, one for each direction, and all that brush and tinder on both sides. It felt like an enormous trap had closed. Or maybe it was that bad times revealed something the people up here didn't want to think about: that we were all in it together, that the danger fell on everyone. Immunity was an illusion; it was impossible to stand apart. When fire swept across the city, it didn't matter where you lived or how much money you had. The flames didn't care, they just burned until the fuel ran out. But in a city like this, where the sprawl inched into wooded hills and canyons like the tendrils of a creeping vine, there was always fuel. *Two-story brush*, the firefighters called it. Houses, in other words. Wood and lathe and furniture and wiring. Tinder cut into shapes we imagined to be safe and solid. But the flames, they never forgot what it really was.

I waited until the driver left before I turned towards the door. The house appeared as impervious, as impenetrable, as it ever had. The windows were shut — *sealed* was the word that came into my mind — and the patio furniture had been enclosed beneath a set of matching slate gray canvas coverings like a gathering of ghosts. You could almost believe the place had been shut up for the winter. Except that winter wouldn't arrive for months. Meanwhile, the ash kept drifting down like some inverted whiteout, warm instead of icy, a blizzard in reverse.

I stood in front of the door with my finger poised above the bell. I could see my reflection in the windows there. Suit a little boxy and red tie hanging low over my belt. I looked like a real estate developer. Or possibly a president. The glass was opaque, or was that just on this side? I had the sudden sense that I was being watched. But how could anyone else see me when I couldn't see myself? My face was a blur above my jacket, like a smear of fingerpaint; it had no clarity or shape. I couldn't see if the worms had grown inflamed from all the heat and smoke. It would be fitting if they had. It would be fitting if they began to bleed again like stigmata. It would be fitting if they gave me away. But they had already given me away, hadn't they? What else to make of the money she had left? Now that money was another thing between us, another secret that we shared.

I straightened my jacket. Then I pressed the bell. I could hear the ringing inside the house, through the vaulted space of the entry hall. At first, there was nothing but its echo, and I wondered if she had evacuated. Why stay in a burning city when you could drive up the coast and ride it out in Ojai or Santa Barbara? There were plenty of places to go if you had the money.

Or at least that's what I'd heard.

I went to push the bell once more, but before I could, the front door opened, and Sylvia was standing in front of me, looking crisp and put together as always, in a knee-length black skirt and ivory silk blouse. She must have been waiting there the whole time, watching me go through my ridiculous little charade on her front steps, waiting for the moment I let down my guard.

"Can I help you?" she said. For a moment, it was as if we'd never met. She made no move to let me in.

"Yes," I answered, and then stopped, uncertain of what to say.

"Come on. Spit it out," she said.

"May I come in?"

"I don't know if I want that. I don't know if that's a good idea."

"I need to ask you about the money. I know about the sequence of the bills."

"Ah, yes," she laughed. "The detective. I keep forgetting about your sleuthing. Well, by all means" — amused now, she threw the door wide open — "please give me the latest on your ... investigation. I couldn't be more intrigued."

I should have left then, but it was a long and smoky trip back down the hill to Hollywood. So I stood there as she laughed at me, eyes flashing not with warmth but something sharper, as if she were probing my skin with a blade. The ash kept falling, and my eyes teared as my throat grew close and scratchy. I didn't want to follow, yet when she turned her back, what choice did I have? Sylvia's heels clicked across that marble chessboard of a floor like a set of small explosions. I knew well enough to stay away. But there were things to get straight, things to sort. There were questions I needed to ask. She had secrets, we all had secrets. I had secrets too. Not for the first time, I understood that we weren't on the same side.

Sylvia led the way into the study and motioned for me to sit. I collapsed into the club chair. The leather smelled clean and crisp but there was no reassurance in it. All it did was remind me that I was an intruder, like the fire and the ash. Or no, not like them — they were part of the ecology. Me, I was an interloper, in this house and everywhere. I was the ghost in the machine, a phantom spirit; I was the element that didn't fit. I had hoped to erase myself, but now look where I was.

In a temperature-controlled room, while outside the hills and canyons burned.

"Look, Sylvia," I said, but she was fussing at the bar, with the bottles and the glasses, spooning out large shards of ice. I almost stopped her, but when I opened my mouth, a sigh of exhaustion emerged instead. I could see Sylvia's back arch slightly at the sound of it, shoulders rising underneath the silk like the stretching of a cat. She turned, her gray eyes sparking, and flashed an insinuating smile.

"Maker's Mark, yes?" she said, crossing the room with a tumbler of brown liquid. I didn't answer, but I took the glass. "I'd join you," she continued, "except you're not going to be here that long."

She stood above me for an instant, rose-lined lips thin and even in the center of her face. Then she arranged herself in the club chair across the table with the self-possession of a cat.

"So," she said, "you had some questions about the money? Something to do with sequencing, you said?"

"Yes," I answered, starting slowly. I hadn't taken a sip of my drink yet, but already I was feeling a loss of control. It was as if the liquor had affected me by osmosis, as if it had atomized into the air. I took a breath and tried to calm my thinking, but my mind was everywhere at once.

"The money," I began again. "The numbers on the bills. The cash you and Corrina gave me both came from the same sequence. I want to ask you about that."

Sylvia's face began to ratchet open, revealing a glimpse of teeth, white and wet inside her mouth. Again, I got the sense of a cat, playing disinterestedly with its prey — a vole, a bird, a house-proud town mouse — before it zeroed in for the kill. I sipped my drink and felt the heat of the liquor in my throat. She was looking at me with expectation, as if she wanted to hear what else I had to say. Then she laughed, a sound so sharp it made me jump, which only caused her to laugh some more.

"That's it?" she said. "That's why you came here?"

"It seems a striking ... anomaly."

"Why, Mister Detective? What do you think it tells you? That my stepdaughter and I are not as estranged as it might seem?"

She sat forward in her chair, smile evaporating as her eyes raked my face.

"As you may or may not understand," she went on, "it's useful for the estate to observe certain protocols until the legalities are resolved. The more reasonable I appear, the better. It helps my case. Or so the lawyers say."

When I didn't answer, she shook her head as if annoyed. "It's very simple. Every month, the estate makes a direct deposit to her bank account. Her apartment is provided too. As for the cash, that's a little something extra. Occasionally, she does a job for me, if we can agree on the details." Again, she laughed, a sound like breaking glass. "Maybe I'm not such a wicked stepmother, after all."

"So the money she gave me came from you?"

"I have no idea what she does with it. Or perhaps I should say what she did." She paused, to focus her thoughts or make me uneasy, I wasn't sure. "As for what she's doing now, I haven't heard from her."

Her eyes searched my face as if for clues.

I knew better than to break her gaze, but silence had descended like a shroud. I could feel it settle over my mouth and nose, like a suffocating hand. It wasn't just this room, but the whole house. White noise, a crypt-like stillness, as if sound itself had ceased to exist. Outside, the city was on fire, and Corrina ... well, Corrina, she was where she was. Here, the air was sealed off, as if we'd removed ourselves from the world. Privilege again, the power of it, the power to imagine an exemption. It was, I realized, how Sylvia had come to live, as if good fortune were an achievement or a choice you made rather than a hand you were dealt.

I wondered what my face was showing. I wondered if the marks revealed my guilt. Like the mark of Cain, condemning him to live as fugitive and wanderer, not unlike the way that I was living now. After murdering Abel, Cain had been cast out. He had become a man without a soul. No one could say, exactly, what the mark looked like, but I wanted to believe that it was residue from the attack.

And yet, for Cain, the mark also meant protection. It was a warning from God, not to Cain but to the others, a guarantee that he would not be killed. This was the part that made no sense, unless the wandering *was* the punishment, unless God was keeping Cain alive to maximize his pain. The very thing that tormented him became the source of his preservation. The Faustian bargain of a duplicitous deity. I couldn't decide which was worse, a god like that or no god at all. In the end, it was just an empty question, for no god had ever revealed its face to me.

I wondered what would happen if I didn't move. I wondered how long I could sit here and stare back at her, as the ice melted in my glass. I wondered if she'd call someone to ease me out, to cart the club chair from the study and deposit it on the lawn. Who would that be? She had to have a staff. No one lived like this without one, but the house was so still, so silent, as if it weren't inhabited at all. It had been that way every time I'd been here, as quiet as a mausoleum, a space in which it felt like a transgression just to take a breath. Where was everyone? Had she sent them home due to the fire? But if so, what about the times before? Were they hiding, waiting for me to make my exit? I wondered how she would react if I got up and started looking, through the foyer to the public rooms and upstairs to where she slept. I imagined parties, people spilling from one space to another, gathering in the study for conversation before moving out to other rooms. Servants would carry drinks on silver trays and pass among the guests, invisible but seeing everything — even after the guests broke into groups of twos and threes and slipped behind closed doors.

Maybe that was how those pictures had been taken, Sylvia and her husband and that unknown other, a party trick, a party favor, a conspiracy or a cabal. I could almost hear them laughing, thinking they were getting away with everything. And they had for a while, until he had died and Corrina had gone crazy and I had gotten involved. Again, I wondered if she knew about the thumb drive, wondered if she had any idea about the images on the internet. All our deceptions, all our fraudulence, eventually it gets revealed. It would happen to me too, at the moment I least expected. It was happening right now. Sylvia's eyes had not left my face, and even as I stared back, I could feel them lacerate me, severing me from everything I had ever dreamt or fantasized about who or what or how I was.

"Are you done," Sylvia asked, "with your questions? Is there anything else you'd like to know? Because, Mister Detective, I have some questions of my own. You want to talk about money? Okay, let's talk about money. The sequences you noticed? Well, a thousand of those dollars came from me. And I expect..."

"Results?" I interjected. My voice sounded thick.

"Results?" She barked out a harsh laugh. "What results could you possibly offer? Look at you in your suit and tie. They don't even fit correctly. Look at you slurping at that drink. No, my friend, all you can provide is information. You know where she is. You and I both understand that. I think it's time for you to stop pretending. Time to face the music, as they say."

In the study, the air felt super-heated, as if the atmosphere were expanding, as if the fire had begun to burn inside the house.

"Do I have anything to worry about?" she asked, enunciating every syllable. It felt like she was speaking to a child. "I don't care about the rest of it. What can you tell me? I expect my money's worth."

Once more, I found myself aware of the weight of the house, its silence. I remembered the first time I saw her, the way she captivated me and kept me off my guard. I still felt out of balance, but the allure, the attraction, had recalibrated as something more like fear. Fear, yes — or better, a desperate kind of wariness, a sense that she could not be trusted, which was also how she thought of me. I wondered why she had let me in, why she was toying with me. I wondered how she wanted this to end. Yes, I knew about Corrina, but I wasn't going to tell her. I didn't want to remember. I wanted to forget.

All of it came down to waiting, all of it came down to letting go. Again, I imagined footmen lurking in those empty rooms, ready to emerge if things became ... untoward. What would I need to do to bring them running? That is, if there was anyone to bring? I hefted the glass in my hand before tipping it back to finish the liquor. Then, I set the empty vessel gently on the table top.

Through it all, I'd held her gaze. It hadn't seemed safe to do otherwise. Now, I lowered my eyes and spoke as evenly as I could manage.

"I'm sorry, Sylvia," I told her. "I've got nothing you can use."

Down in Hollywood, the air was cleaner. Or maybe it was a different kind of dirt. Here in the flats, the fire seemed far off, backgrounded, less an active glow than a muted wash. People went about their business with a studied nonchalance. It was only when you looked into their eyes that you could see it: that unconscious twitching, the kind that said the future was uncertain, snapping like a metronome.

My place felt as still as Sylvia's had been, everything as it had been left. On the table was a glass, as if transposed from up the hill, still painted with the stain of my last drink. I thought I might have another; it was early but what else did I have going on? I went to the kitchen to retrieve the bottle, and that was when I heard it: a wet noise, ragged, not unlike a sob.

The sound was close, behind me almost, but when I turned there was only emptiness. Through the window shades, I could see the creeping residue of day. It made me uncomfortable, so opaque and tenuous. It felt tainted in some way. I strained to pierce the silence, to get beneath the surface and hear its hidden frequencies. At first, there was nothing, but then I heard it once more, not quite at the level of a whisper. As I listened, the intonation took on the textures of my name.

My name? I thought about the last time this had happened.

But no, it couldn't be.

I looked toward the bedroom. The door was closed. I did not remember leaving it that way. It made me feel as if I'd been caught, as if there was no possibility of escape. I inched across the carpet, footsteps silent and unheard. It was as if I had become a ghost in my own apartment, as if I no longer made a mark. At the door, I paused to collect myself. I could feel anxiety rise across the surface of my skin. Every nerve ending felt electrified, as if my body had been turned inside out.

Up close, the noise was clearer. There was no doubt it was directed at me. I wrapped my fingers around the handle and pulled the door back. The bedroom air was dark and fecund, like a catacomb had been unsealed. Sweat and sleep and bodily secretions, and underneath all that, another scent, or set of scents: loam and lichen and kerosene, the bitter breath of burning wood.

No, I thought, *it couldn't be*. Or did I speak those words aloud? My eyes could not adjust. All I could see were shapes — the boxy outline of the bureau, the flattened platform of the bed. Then, the quarter light grew sharper, and I made out a different sort of silhouette. There was a disruption in the bed, under the comforter, what looked like a form, a body. That was where the sound was coming from.

I raised my hand to click on the lights, but something kept me from pressing the switch. It wasn't that I didn't want to know, but it seemed safer this way. From the bed, the rasp of ragged breathing. I took a step into the room. My only plan was to move quickly. I wanted this to be like pulling off a scab. Another step and then another, and I was at the bedside. I reached down, grabbed the covering and pulled it off, terrified to look but unwilling to avert my eyes.

114

Corrina was crouching on the mattress, although it was hard to say where she ended and the bed began. She no longer seemed to possess physical boundaries, exactly; her body had maintained its shape and structure, but she was bleeding out along the edges like the flicker of a fading signal, a transmission that had reached the end point of its range. This was not an aura, not ectomorphic residue. She was not a spirit or a soul. If I were to touch her, I had the sense that I would encounter a solid body, that my hand would rest on flesh and bone. Her skin was mottled, red and green and scarred in places, but otherwise intact. *How?* I thought — and then her eyes snapped open, and I didn't think about anything for a while.

Those eyes, they were quicksilver, with neither pupil nor iris; no lavender as they mirrored my own image back at me. The marks on my cheeks flared in their reflection, bright red like tiny licks of fire. I could hear my name through her ragged breathing, but she was not speaking in any way I understood. Her mouth remained shut and her face bore no expression, and she did not seem aware of my presence — or, for that matter, of her own.

"Corrina?" I said, but it was less a question than an identifying remark. It was as if I were looking at a lineup — of suspects, perhaps, or her corpse lying in the morgue. She had to be identified; how would I know what this was if I couldn't name it? How would I know how to react? I should have just walked away, lit another match and torched the bungalow with her inside it. But I was in too deep.

"Corrina?" I said again, and she turned those empty eyes my way. It felt like I was drowning in their maelstrom. It felt like my soul was being consumed. I could feel the heat closing in, same as at Sylvia's, and I wondered if there was something else between them, something more, and weirder, than either had let on. Maybe she had been there, at her stepmother's. Maybe it had been Corrina, or her specter, concealed behind one of those closed doors, waiting for me to make my move.

Well, I had made my move and now here I was,

in a situation I didn't know how to recognize. It was all I could do to keep my feet as Corrina rose up, and a spit of flame emerged from her eyes. Her body seemed to be expanding. Its weight and breadth consumed the bed. The odor in the room grew thick with decomposition; I could see her skin begin to peel and curl. Beneath its blistered surface, I could make out the bones of her jaw and the long shape of her tongue, blackened as if by fire.

"I'm sorry," I said, but I didn't mean it. We both knew it didn't matter anyway. As I spoke, she drifted towards me until for the first time, she seemed to regard me, although I could not imagine what she saw. Then, from out of that broken face, she began to laugh — a long ululating roar that rose and modulated like a conflagration, crackling and raging as it burned out of the canyon and all the way across the city, only to end up in the very spot it had begun.

"Stop," I said, but she didn't appear to hear me. Or maybe we were on two different planes. "Corrina, please" — and now I was aware that I was moaning, that my body had grown rigid with fear. It was only a matter of time before someone heard her, or … The possibilities were beyond what I could comprehend. I, who believed in nothing, who thought the universe was a vicious joke. That was still true, I supposed, but the joke had turned on me. She was laughing because she knew it, because she knew I couldn't get away. She was laughing because it was she who had condemned me, from the moment I first heard her scream.

The air was close now, suffocating, as if she had sucked up all the oxygen. My lungs constricted as I gasped for air. Black moths began to flutter at the edges of my vision. When they got to the center, it would be too late. For a moment, I almost gave in to the inevitable. For a moment, I almost let it go. It had been so long, such a hard time, and I was so tired. Why not just allow myself to be swept away? It would be a fitting end, the evaporation of everything, and I would be gone, at last, excised from the world. That was what I wanted, the release of it, the easing up, the freedom, death as liberation or release.

Yet death was not a liberation. Corrina's presence confirmed that. No, death was just another struggle, another source of pain. I don't know what else I'd expected. I don't know what I'd hoped to find. There was no God; there was no salvation. I had gone too far to be saved.

Still, there was survival. The desire for it screamed from every cell in my body; it curled my hand into a fist. I didn't know if I was screaming when I did it. I just knew I was screaming after it was done. As Corrina laughed, I drew back my arm and swung at her, a roundhouse that caught her jaw and passed right through. Her body was not solid, as I had imagined. It was a floating mix of vapors as diaphanous, as evanescent, as a set of veils. The realization made me scream even more as my fist connected with the wall, and I felt the plaster yield.

And now I felt myself falling, as if into an open grave. The grave was my bed and it was empty; Corrina was gone. From a ghost to a ghost, a hallucination to a hallucination. Not a trace of her remained.

I was alone here. I had always been alone here.

I had always been alone.

QUESTION NUMBER TEN:
CAN WE GET IN?

I woke up feeling empty. I woke up feeling brutalized. Or no, not brutalized, not exactly. More the way you feel after a fever has passed. There was that wrung-out aspect, the sense that my body had been drained. And then, the other — looser, harder to pin down, something that, I wanted to imagine, seemed a bit like peace.

I wasn't sure what had happened. I didn't know if she was real. What I did know was that I had gotten through it. I had faced the maelstrom and come out the other side. My bedroom was a mess — sheets and blankets strewn about, a fist-sized hole impressed into the wall. I remembered my fist, the point of impact. I remembered how it had passed right through her, how the biggest surprise had been her incorporeality. I had been expecting her to be … human. I had been expecting a physical form. I had not imagined she would come to me in some other, evanescent state, as fleeting and insubstantial as smoke drifting through the air.

And smoke was nothing I couldn't handle. Smoke had been buffeting Los Angeles for days. I wondered if she had returned to the vortex. Either way, in the filtered half-light of morning, she was not my problem anymore.

That hole in the wall, though … it grinned at me like a mouth. The plaster had caved in around the edges, leaving a fractured leer that looked like it was full of broken teeth. If I waited long enough, would it begin speaking? What would it have to say? I was out along the edge now, beyond the bounds of human reckoning, in the territory where the mystery asserts itself. I knew enough to recognize that this would yield no answers. I knew that it would give me nothing I could use. The mystery. Enigma was more like it. Every time I found myself in its presence, I was forced to stare down not understanding but its opposite — the roiling chaos at the heart of everything.

Even now, that mouth was whispering in my direction. The sound was too low to be distinct. It brought me back to another bedroom, another home, the one I'd occupied with my wife. During the final days, after our quixotic attempts at reconciliation, she had sent me to camp out on the couch. I had tried so hard to forget this, to purge it not just from memory but also consciousness. And yet, there it was, in the flutter of an eyelid, a thing that cannot be erased. I remembered one night — our last? — pounding on the bedroom door until its wooden surface splintered, throwing my body hard against the lock. I could no longer say what was on the other side, what I had found there. I could no longer say who I was.

Was that what the mouth was trying to tell me? Was that what the mouth was whispering? In the kitchen, I rummaged for a roll of duct tape in the utility drawer. Taping up the hole felt as if I were muzzling someone, as if I were shutting off both breath and speech. I began with one strip, and added another and another until the effect was like an impasto, projecting out of the wall into three-dimensional space. I spackled on a fourth layer and a fifth one; I added tape until the roll was done. Back in the kitchen, I retrieved a red Sharpie, which I used to adorn the clotted tape with a garish, leering set of lips.

There, I thought, or said aloud. It didn't look like Corrina, but that was not the point.

I kept the door wide open when I left the bedroom. I wanted everything exposed. Through the windows I could hear the sound of commotion. Or no: the sound of industry. When I pulled back the corner of the curtain, Sylvia was on the steps of Corrina's unit, talking to three day workers — from the Home Depot on Sunset, unless I missed my guess. The front door lay open, revealing the emptiness within. John, the property manager, was there also, in blue shorts and tee shirt, the clothing of an outsized child. He looked like a child, too, as Sylvia talked to him, an unhappy child with eyes downcast and mouth tightened into a pout as if she were giving him instructions, or dressing him down. This was a posture I didn't recognize; with him, it was usually the other way around.

I could feel my breath grow sharp and tight.

Sylvia was twenty feet away, although it may as well have been twenty miles. I watched as she spoke. I couldn't make out the words but the tone was clear. Confident, directed, not sharp although it could easily turn. I'd been on the receiving end of that voice each time we had been together. It was the voice one used when talking to the help. I'd never heard her speak differently to anyone. Now, she spoke to John, and he spoke to the workers. It was like watching a chain of command. The men listened and moved into the apartment. Something about it didn't add up.

I drew back the curtain to get a wider angle. I wanted to see if anyone else was there. The sunlight glinted off the glass, arresting me with its reflection. It was pale but pointed, yellow and no longer brown. I knew what that meant, although it wasn't what I had expected. It meant the fire was being brought under control. It was only a matter of time before the hot spots were extinguished and investigators started swarming Malibu, looking for the flashpoint, for evidence that might be left behind. I became aware of the sound of my own breathing: raspy, raw, as if I had the flu. The flu, yes ... or some respiratory virus. It felt as unreal to me as a fever reverie.

Then Sylvia looked up, as if she had seen me, as if she were aware of being observed. Her gray eyes sharpened and she turned towards the window behind which I was standing, off to the side and out of view. In the daylight, I knew, I was pretty much invisible. I had stood out in the courtyard more than once, looking at this window. All I could see was the refracted image of the sky. I tried to imagine it from her perspective: a wash of cloud cover bunched like gauze as it moved lightly across the facing surface of the glass. And yet, that didn't match her gaze, which was piercing, as if a hawk had landed on Corrina's steps. Her chin was finely etched, as if carved from marble; it would be, I imagined, cold to the touch. Her nose was refined and narrow, hair swept back in a loose chignon. The style accentuated her long neck and the line of her body, which curved beneath her tailored skirt and blouse like a single muscle, taut as a raptor's wing. I could sense her narrowing her focus, trying to peer inside. She knew I lived here, knew I had nowhere else to be, I felt my blood rise. She held herself with predatory grace.

I tried to meet her gaze, but I couldn't do it, even through the window frame. Instead, my eyes moved to the hibachi, which remained on the steps. All of a sudden, I wanted to have it, as a keepsake, or a way of keeping track. I had been there, after all, on those steps, just as I had been inside. As I watched, Sylvia sniffed the air, as if for smoke, and looked my way once more. I imagined that I could see her calculating, toting up the evidence, making deductions. I dropped the curtain and stepped back into the room.

It would take hours to clear out Corrina's place. I had no idea whether Sylvia would stay for all of it, although I hoped not. I didn't want to face her. I didn't want her to knock on my door. The push and pull was overwhelming. I had the feeling that if I let down my guard, even for a moment, she would swallow me alive.

And what about John? That was something else I was going to need to ponder, another piece of evidence, another clue.

In the living room, I put on some music. Then I poured a drink. I had no idea what time it was, but time — the a.m. and the p.m. of it, anyway — was no longer relevant to me. It had ceased to be measurable by any known demarcations; it had become a flood, a fire. Everything seemed to be happening at once, and the only way to deal with that was to let it carry me, to give in and go for the ride.

Through the speakers, I could hear the opening pattern of Elmore James's "Shake Your Moneymaker." I had listened to this song so often, with its repeated lyric, the simplest thing in the world, you'd think. But that didn't explain the nuance, the drive of it. That didn't explain the appeal. I thought of Elmore, dead in Chicago of a heart attack at forty-five. I had always imagined him struck down beneath the thunder and the pouring rain. The sky is crying, he had sung, but this was Southern California, which meant that, for most of the year, the sky withheld its tears. Only in the winter months did it allow itself to be unburdened, in torrents of elemental force. This winter, the rain would tear up Malibu, picking up where the fires had left off. The water would pour through the canyons, taking houses and hillsides and whatever else might have been lost or buried along the way. Each was an erasure. Each allowed us to forget. It was this forgetting that kept us going. It was this forgetting that led us to believe, against all other indications, that we were blessed.

Outside, the workers banged and chattered at their labor. Or was that just the whining of their cleaning machines? Either way, when they were done, this too would be washed away, another erasure, another flood. Corrina would be gone without a trace. In a way, it was like finishing the job that I had started, or no — the job Corrina had started, that she had set in motion. I needed to remember; it had all begun with her. Without Corrina, I wouldn't be in this situation. Without Corrina, I would have never been involved. Now, I was hiding out in my apartment, hoping that Sylvia would leave me alone. I wanted to erase her also, or at least my knowledge of her. I wanted one of us — either Sylvia or me — to disappear.

Then, the song shifted into the first verse, and there it was — one more whisper, one more echo in the long history of the blues.

Well, I got a girl, she lives up on the hill

From Pete Johnson to Elmore James, from 1938 to 1961. That was the span between two lifetimes ... not unlike Sylvia's and Corrina's, you might say. I couldn't help but imagine that, were I to pull back the curtain, Sylvia would be standing with her face against the window, waiting on the other side of the glass.

I willed myself not to get up and look. Instead, I opened my laptop to check for updates on the fire. It was now more than forty percent contained, which explained the limpid quality of the light. The winds had shifted away from the city, leaving the flames to burn themselves out in the brush. I ought to have felt relieved, I understood that. But I didn't. More like a reckoning was coming due.

I needed to sort through the information. I needed to figure out where I was. I went to the bedroom, avoiding the taped-up hole with its garish lips. That was a wormhole I didn't want to go down. It was a maw that could devour me. I took up the envelope of money. I found Corrina's 5150 intake form. A party, a knife, a threat to stab the host. It sounded like a Leadbelly song. And where did all this leave me? Corrina had been unstable, I understood that. She'd been to rehab twice. I thought about her apartment, all that furniture. It had been a project, I suddenly realized, or at least intentional. The imposition of order, or at least illusion, as a kind of firewall. Maybe she'd been fending off the darkness. Maybe she'd been trying to keep the madness at bay. I wondered what it might have been like for her, alone in the middle of the night. I wondered what it might have been like when she screamed. I had experienced such nights also. I had never stopped experiencing them. Dark night of the soul ... it was a cliché. But it was also a reality. Every cliché was in the end. We called them clichés because we didn't want to face them, didn't want to acknowledge what they implied. We wanted our lives to be more complex. We wanted to be unique. Yet late at night was when eternity contracted, until you couldn't stand to remain in your body for a second more. You needed everything to be finished. I had been there. Now, I was on the edge of being there again.

Back in the living room, "Shake Your Moneymaker" was winding down. Elmore and his band, the Broomdusters, had been known to stretch the song to thirty minutes when they performed it, vamping their audiences into a frenzy. I imagined them in some South Side juke joint, ceiling low and close above the stage. There would be the smell of sweat and pheromones and whiskey, Saturday night yielding to Sunday morning, prayer to another kind of prayer. *See you in church*, the bartender used to say to me. Each was sacred in its way. Even so, neither one could save us. Neither one could bring us back. All those people dancing and drinking and playing music, on some lost evening in the middle of a distant century. How many of them remained among the living? Not many, I would wager. As for the others, they might as well have never been born for all the good it did them now.

And yet, I thought, as I withdrew the hundred dollar bills: shake your moneymaker indeed. I had been doing that since I'd met Corrina, since the night she knocked on my door. When had that been, that first encounter? It felt like years, but it had only been a week or two. I tried to count the days back, but it was too hard. Instead, I picked up the intake form. She had been taken to Harbor-UCLA, a public hospital, and kept under observation for three days. The photocopy was blurry, difficult to read, scratched out in a hasty scrawl. The checked boxes on the second page, however, were as irrefutable as they had ever been:

> *A danger to himself / herself*
> *A danger to others*

Well, that had been the case, hadn't it? She had been a danger to us both. Now she had re-emerged as a tulpa: a sign of madness, or an emanation from the border between worlds. I felt harassed, I felt possessed and haunted. There had to be something I could do. I opened a search window and looked up: *How do I get rid of a tulpa?* It took half a dozen websites before I found what I was looking for. *Have no shame*, it instructed. *It's the things you feel shameful about that they'll use against you. You are an animal born of chaos in a ruined and corrupting world.*

Well, yes, I understood this. It was certainly true. But no shame? What did that look like? Although I did all I could to push my shame away. Stuff it down, try not to remember.

Keep the doubt — the *fear* — at bay.

It was solipsism again, of course it was. But the tulpa was a challenge. The tulpa was an assault. Its presence asserted something I didn't want to accept, that I couldn't control what I'd projected, that I was the source of my own chaos, that it had everything to do with me. As for strategies of disengagement, the website suggested avoiding alcohol and general disorder. I laughed as I took a long pull off my drink.

Listening to music was advised.

That was easy. I had been listening to music when I met her. I was listening to music now. As I scrolled through the website, Robert Johnson's "32-20 Blues" began to throb softly like a whisper from another world:

> *Aha, baby, where you stayed last night*
> *Aha, baby, where you stayed last night*
> *You got your hair all tangled and you ain't talking right*

It was as good a description as any of what I'd seen.

And yet, music hadn't helped repel the tulpa. Music had seemed to compel her instead. As for the rest of it, what did it have to do with how I lived? I'd come looking for a spell or an invocation. I'd come looking for a spiritual fix. But whoever had developed these solutions was living in a different world.

Then I caught sight of one more entry, at the bottom of the screen. It referred to humus, and at first, I thought it was a recipe. The spelling, however, it was different; not *hummus*, but without the second *m*. Such an inconsequential distinction, a rounding error. Until I read a little further and realized I was wrong.

This humus was not a foodstuff. It was an organic substance like compost, a dark material produced by decomposing animal or vegetable matter, necessary for soil fertility. From life to death to life again, a form of transmutation, transfiguration, transmigration, transubstantiation … and wasn't that what I was after too? I didn't have any humus and I didn't know where to find it. But I did have an idea.

I went to the refrigerator. There was some hummus in a crusty tub in the back. I couldn't say when I had bought it, but I didn't care if it was still good to eat. Transubstantiation, yes — from hummus to humus, from food to some elemental residue. I grabbed the tub, and the bottle of Maker's, after topping off my glass.

In the bedroom, I took a sip of whiskey, then poured a little on my fingers, and smeared it across the lips I'd drawn. From outside, I could hear the workers, all their moving and their cleaning, reverberating beneath the breathstrokes of the music, not unlike a rhythm track. I could hear another voice, a man's voice, cutting through the racket, giving orders. It sounded like John. In the living room, the music maintained its low, amorphous hum. I rubbed more liquor on the mouth to the competing downbeats. I took a pull of Maker's and swirled it on my tongue.

The mouth, it kept on leering, more so now that it was drunk. I dug another finger deep into the hummus, and thought again about the double meaning of the word. Things were never what they looked like, were they? Things were never how they appeared. The glob felt cool on my skin, like a soothing plaster; I began to spread it on the wall. I created lines that took the shape of a head, with those lips at its center. The face was less full than Corrina's, more angular and severe. I could almost feel its gray eyes piercing. I could almost hear the sharpness of its voice. Could it be that I had missed a key connection, that it wasn't Corrina who was the tulpa? Maybe the tulpa had been right outside my window. Maybe the tulpa was still around.

I don't know how long I stayed in the bedroom. I only know that it was twilight when I emerged. None of the lights were on in my apartment, but as I inched through the grayness of the living room, I could hear the day workers, still on the job. They kept moving in and out of the apartment. They kept talking back and forth. I wondered how much Sylvia had paid them. Not enough, that was for sure. Just a few hundred dollars, in sequential bills. I could almost guess what the numbers were. I clicked off the sound system and gathered myself in the gloaming. Then I tiptoed to the window and inched the curtain back.

Outside, night was falling, and Sylvia was nowhere to be seen.

I waited until after midnight. I waited to find out what it was all about. I waited for hours, sipping whiskey in the silence, until the workers had packed up and the courtyard had gone still. I waited until my eyes adjusted and I could see through the darkness, until I had become a Dark Watcher once again. Then I crept to the door and slid down the steps, moving on Corrina's place like some sort of vapor in the blankness, some sort of emanation in the night.

The crew had turned off the lights but left the door unlocked. I looked around before I tried the handle — there was no one watching — and let myself inside. The furniture had been carted off and the whole apartment, from what I could make out, had been scrubbed and disinfected; when I laid my hand against one of the walls, it came away bearing a faint scent of pine.

I spent a while in the front room, avoiding the bedroom at the back. The door was ajar, but I was afraid to go back there. Maybe someone was waiting — Sylvia, with the police, or John, or those phantom footmen. Or Corrina, back from wherever it was that she had gone. I felt myself coming unstuck from my body. Just to move through these rooms was like returning to the scene of a crime.

The hibachi was still on the front step, a witness. The only lingering reminder of what had happened, of how the place had once been occupied. In a few weeks, a month, a new tenant would move in, bringing new furniture and a new set of concerns. Until then, the apartment would remain stripped to its barest essence, walls and floors and doors and windows: an empty template, waiting for someone — anyone — to fill it in. It was a husk, a body after the soul had been removed.

I had been a part of that, I supposed.

But after a few minutes, my disquiet faded. I almost felt as if I belonged. It was like I was, again, invincible, exterminating angel or otherwise. Through the front door I could hear the sound of crickets; I could smell the jasmine as it bloomed. In the middle of the city, darkness wasn't really darkness; it took on its own sodium-inflected glow. Narrow tendrils of orange light eclipsed the shadows. They made me feel as if there was nothing that I could not see.

"Hello?" I said, emboldened.

The silence of the apartment answered me.

I walked through the kitchen and the bathroom. I trailed my fingers on the countertops. My mind felt lighter, freer. It was as if the tulpa had disappeared. Humus, hummus, the difference of a single letter. Perhaps it had been close enough. Either way, for this moment anyhow, it seemed I'd found a respite of sorts.

At the front window, I looked into the courtyard. I could see my apartment to the left. Windows dark behind their curtains. Another set of rooms devoid of life. This must have been where she had stood when she was screaming. The first few times, at any rate. I could picture her here, in her ankle boots and skinny jeans, trying to look like every other young woman her age.

That had been a dodge, though, hadn't it? That had been a lie. I knew something of what it felt like, to have your insides and your outsides discontinuous. I was aware of it every time I stepped into the world. I was aware of it right now. It was why I had worn a suit when I'd gone up the hill to see Sylvia — not because it made me feel as if I belonged, but because it reminded me I never could.

The stain of complicity, of sin, of my *responsibility*, it was too great.

But now, I wanted that responsibility. Now, I wanted to assert who I was. I had nothing to be scared of. It was all done and gone. I moved from the window to the bedroom, and pushed against the door. These walls had been scrubbed clean also. The scent of ammonia burned the inside of my nose.

I walked the edges of the room as if pacing off its dimensions. It was important not to lose track of the physical. You could get into trouble if you stopped believing certain principles. You could get lost in a dreamscape of your own. That had happened to me also, when I was married, and I could see how it might happen now again. One step, two steps, three steps ... all the way along one wall until I reached a corner, at which point I turned and counted more.

It was while I was doing this that I saw it. Or sensed it — that's more the way it was. The closet door was open and it was darker here, away from the courtyard. But I could tell that something had been left here, something for me to find. I stepped into the closet and tried to see my way through the floating particles of night. Nothing at first, then a dull glint beckoning against a back wall, flickering at me. I bent to retrieve it, closed my fingers around what turned out to be a small square shape. Metal, encased in what felt like melted plastic. It felt familiar, but I couldn't place it.

And then I knew.

It was the thumb drive, although how it had gotten here I couldn't say. I might have been screaming as I ran from the apartment. I didn't remember getting home.

Back at my place, I locked the doors and windows. I did not turn on the lights. I opened my laptop and in the glow of the screen, I could see it: the same solid state component, the molded plastic scorched from the fire. The tulpa, of course. The tulpa was still here. And I had deluded myself. I was in too deep, and it was going to take more than a single set of spells or incantations to fight my way back out.

I plugged the zip drive into my computer, but it was too damaged to be read. Before I withdrew it, however, I thought I saw the lingering afterimage of a face. A woman's face, severe and stark, with the gray eyes I had come to know so well. I could feel them burning into me like acid. I could feel the fire on my skin. I flung the drive across the room as if it were molten. What the fuck? What had I gotten myself into? Where did I go from here?

The obvious answer was the bottle, which remained on the table. I poured a healthy slug into my glass. It was only when I looked up that I noticed the window on my browser, which was open to a news site featuring updates on the fire.

BREAKING NEWS, its headline screamed in capital letters. I could almost hear the shouting in the room. A body had been recovered in Malibu. The location was a canyon investigators had identified as a potential starting point.

It was the first fatality of the fire, the article concluded. But I knew that wasn't true. How could it be the fire's fault if the body had been dead already?

I stared at the screen and took another drink.

QUESTION NUMBER ELEVEN:
IT'LL BE JUST LIKE HEAVEN?

People like to tell you it will be better in the morning. People like to say you just have to get through the night. I once watched an interview with someone who had attempted suicide; "If I could have only imagined getting past the next minute," he told the television reporter, "I never would have tried to kill myself." The problem was the present. It existed without a future or a past. In that eternal ongoing moment, there was no hope of resolution. There was no relief.

I didn't want to look at the computer. But I couldn't turn away. Throughout that whole long night of darkness, I kept hitting refresh on my browser, but it didn't show me anything new. One more kind of static present. One more instant in which time had stopped. Yet unlike the night I'd driven to Malibu, this sense of suspended time was anything but reassuring. I was burning up with worry. Or was that fear?

It's not that I thought anyone would find me. Not the authorities, at any rate. The corporeal world did not concern me; there were too many broken strings and inconsistencies, too many disconnected ends. No one was really looking for Corrina. It was in all our interests that she remain unfound. Once the fire was extinguished, I would go back up the hill to visit Sylvia and I would tell her there was nothing to concern her. I would tell her I had watched as Corrina drove away.

As for the body, there was no identifying information, nothing to connect us. We had lived in the same bungalow court, that was all. We had been together a handful of times, most right here in this living room. If anyone asked, I would admit it. What was wrong with anything we'd done? It didn't mean anything ... or at least, it wasn't supposed to. Although that had never been the way it played out.

But then there was the tulpa, and I didn't know what to do about that. This was not corporeal, it was the way of madness, a low, simmering heat that started behind my eyeballs, and sizzled out along my fingers and my toes. In its grip, I couldn't get comfortable. In its grip, I couldn't sit still. Every few minutes, I would get up and patrol the apartment, checking the rooms under cover of the darkness, peering into all the closets and the drawers.

That was the problem with the tulpa, you never knew where or how she would manifest. I dabbed another clot of hummus around the face I had sketched out in the bedroom, although with the lights off, it was impossible to see the effect. Then I retrieved the bottle and sat on the bed for a while drinking from it, occasionally dabbing a few drops gently on her mouth. Better to keep her happy. Better to keep her calm. Maybe if she were inebriated, she would hold to herself, stay out of my business. It had mostly worked that way for me.

The drinking put me into something of a stupor. Or maybe it just defused the urgency. I didn't know the hour and I didn't want to. I had no place to be. I had succeeded, finally, in severing myself from everything; the body in the canyon was proof of that. Now that it had been discovered, I was permanently on the other side. I was Stack O'Lee, a man who stood outside the law. But Stack O'Lee had been gunned down in an act of vigilante justice. All I wanted was to hide.

This had happened with my wife also. The longer we had been together, the more I'd receded. After she was gone, I stayed in our townhome for a week or two, and then I left it behind. It was not my name on the title. It was not my name on the deed. Everything had belonged to her and there was no inheritance. California is a community property state, but I never saw her face again.

And it's true that I had certain ... remedies. But those remedies would put me too much in the light. I preferred to linger in the darkness, as I was doing tonight. I'd kept the money in our cash accounts. I'd taken the stereo.

Better to make a clean break, to start anew, as if I had no history. Better to forget the past.

Where would I go now? I wondered about that as I drank. California was big, and there were many places I could lose myself. I had that envelope full of hundreds. It wasn't enough, but it would get me started. I still had a bit of money in the bank.

Yet even as I dreamt this, I knew it wouldn't happen, just as it hadn't happened with my wife. I had vanished, yes, in a manner of speaking. I had run to ground. I had hidden out so long I had forgotten I was hiding. I had come to believe it was a way of life. But it wasn't a way of life, it was a way of dying, and even the pieces I'd held onto, like the money and the music, echoed at me from beyond the grave.

By now, the gray light of dawn was beginning to trickle through the gaps around the curtains; it was pale and translucent as a watercolor wash. I rubbed my eyes and made a pot of coffee, laced it with the Maker's Mark. I sat at the computer and refreshed the news site. Then I refreshed it again. There was nothing, but I kept clicking anyway, as if by force of will I could provoke some sort of revelation, as if my belief — or my desire — would make the information come to life.

I clicked through to another website, and then a third one, and a fourth. At some point, I must have dozed because when I returned to the world, or to myself, it was midmorning, the light diffuse and soupy in that Southern California summer way. I went to the door and looked out; the sky was flat and without ceiling, striated with the barest ruffle of cirrus clouds. The heat was already an assault. Overhead, a feather-shaped cloud pointed down at me like a finger, an identifying mark.

I closed the door and poured a cup of coffee. I could taste the whiskey beneath the bitter alkaline. Then I noticed the zip drive in the corner, where it had landed during the night. In the daylight, I could see the damage: plastic melted like cooled lava, metal casing seared and scorched. It was the drive I'd removed from Sylvia's study

133

— either that or a remarkable facsimile. I retrieved it and felt my breath rise; I had no idea how it had gotten back to me. What did Sylvia know? And if it was she who had left it, what did she want with me? To send a message, surely, or a reminder, to let me know how much she understood. At the same time, she had done me a favor, returning a piece of evidence, something that might incriminate me.

Or no, I thought, staring at the drive again — it wasn't me who might be incriminated. The images on this drive, they implicated her. I clicked through to the site where I'd uploaded them, searched until I found the link. No one had looked in days, it seemed, the numbers as unchanged as the digits on a broken clock. It had been only a week or two since I had watched the viewer count rise in real time. Now, the traffic had gone as stagnant as standing water. I clicked on the first image and watched it fill the screen.

There it was again, Corrina's father. And Sylvia with the whip. The rich are different from you and me, although what struck me was not the difference but the similarity. My wife and I, we had engaged in our own games. In the end, they became all we had. Now I was alone, looking at pictures of another couple, one of whom was dead. One instant he'd been breathing and the next his heart had stopped. I wondered if Sylvia was with him. I wondered if they'd been doing this.

Quickly, I scrolled through the pictures. At the end of the sequence, I came to the one where his face went red, as if it were bursting; I could see his eyes press out above the gag. What if this was the moment of his dying? What if I'd posted another piece of evidence? I enlarged the image, trying to peer inside it, but there was no way to pierce the surface of the screen.

I reduced the size once more and went back to the beginning. This time, I looked not at the action but at the shadows, the angle of the lens. Yes, it was certainly hand-held, the framing different with every photo, every parallax. I could almost trace the movements of the shooter, always in front of the couple but in more than one instance shadowed by the light. I tried to zero in on those shadows. I tried to see what they revealed. I had the sense that if I could figure this out I'd have the key to everything, that the mystery would be resolved.

But that was ridiculous, wasn't it? There was no mystery here. He had died, whether on this night or another, and his daughter had hired me. I had nothing to do with any of it. I didn't take responsibility at all. What they did on their own time was their business. I was just the conduit.

And what about John? What was his part? That was another question to be resolved. I kept seeing Sylvia, out in the courtyard, talking to him as if he were her servant. Her servant ... or her employee. I clicked on the management company website, but his name was the only point of contact. It was like staring at a wall. Then, I did a public records search. Twenty-five dollars for the basics: property reports, liens, deed histories, owner information. Something was here, an itch, a loose end, a misremembered detail. Who was to say what was important? Who was to say what was a necessary thread?

I skipped over the first three items; what did I care how much the complex cost? But the owners, that was a different matter, as I understood as soon as I discovered who they were. It should have been obvious, I should have known it, there was only one way it could have played out. There it was in black and white, staring back at me across the circuits. Two names: Sylvia Glenn and her late husband, Corrina's father. As exposed as I had made them on the fetish site.

Here was the explanation, or part of it — the part about Corrina screaming, the part about her not held to account. *Her apartment is provided*, Sylvia had told me, although as with so much else, I'd misunderstood. She was into them for all of it, or vice versa. She and Sylvia had remained enmeshed. Her father had bought the complex. It was one of his real estate deals. And me? I was damned now. The details didn't matter, that was just a narrative. The real story, it had no purpose. It had no hook, no epiphany. Nobody ever learned anything. So many secrets. I'd been trapped from the moment I moved in.

I closed the laptop and finished the coffee. When I stood, I faltered for a moment, head light and body out of balance. It was the Maker's and the closed-up air of the apartment. It was the tension of the last several days. I had to change the framework, the perspective. I had to seek another lens. In the bathroom, I washed my face and checked myself in the mirror. The scratches were nearly gone. Or at least, they had receded. They were difficult to see.

I brushed my teeth and put on clean clothes. I forced myself to eat a piece of bread. As I retrieved my wallet from the bureau in the bedroom, I caught a flicker of movement at the edge of my vision, but when I turned, there was just the tulpa, those lips and the outline of a face, crusted and smeared. The tub of hummus sat where I had left it on the mattress. Unrefrigerated, it had begun to smell. I reached in and scooped out the remaining contents. The clot of it felt clay-like in my palm.

For a moment, I stared at that mouth, as if expecting to hear it speak. Then I coated the tape and the surrounding wall with hummus until the tulpa was obscured. Flecks of food spattered the mattress and congealed along the wall. In the stale air of the room, it was as if it had already begun to fester, as if the dark organic material had already begun to form. My eyes watered at the pungency but it seemed a necessary ritual. If I'd remembered any prayers, I might have muttered one.

I put on my shoes and left the bedroom, leaving the door ajar. It was ten thirty in the morning when I stepped into the courtyard.

Above my head, the sky was translucent. The clouds had burned away. The heat was immediate, pressing against me like a physical force. I did a quick reconnaissance: Corrina's place remained empty. Everything else was quiet, as if all the other residents had moved away. Maybe they were at work or maybe not. I had no idea what day it was. Was anybody watching? What did it matter anyway? I ducked my head and sidled down the path to the sidewalk, where I began to walk towards central Hollywood.

Los Angeles is not a walking city. That's another cliché of the place. It plays out in movies and the kind of newspaper think pieces that don't require a lot of thought. But if it's hard to walk here, you can do it — and I did. I was not like the walker, on some strange internal pilgrimage, tracing and retracing my steps through the side streets of the city, as if I were walking a dreamscape into being. I walked for necessities, to pick up groceries, to go to the liquor store. I may not have had a car since I'd been with my wife, but I could get myself wherever I needed to go.

Today, I didn't need to get anywhere. I just needed to get away. I wanted to get lost, to put a little distance between myself and everything.

I wanted to remove myself from my own world.

And what better way to do that than to remove myself from the apartment? What better way to hide than not to hide at all? I followed Franklin to Highland, past the church with the red AIDS ribbon on its bell tower. I thought about going inside, but there was nothing there for me. Instead, I crossed and turned east on Yucca, into the neighborhood north of Hollywood Boulevard. All those 1920s apartments rising above the narrow streets: no lights, no stars, no Walk of Fame. Hollywood had surprised me when I'd first arrived here. I had been expecting something else. Not elegance but maybe history. You could find some of that on the Boulevard, Musso & Frank, the Chinese Theatre ... but it was all still part of the show.

Along these streets, however, it was different. The history felt real. These buildings had stood for a century; they had seen life and death and desolation; they had seen degradation and despair. I tried to imagine Hollywood before they were constructed, a bunch of frame houses on the interurban line. The image flickered like a silent movie before it faded to gray. Who knew what Hollywood had been then? In some sense, it must have always been like this. A place with people going through the motions. A place with people trying to make it through the day.

A block or two ahead, I could see another person on the sidewalk. Otherwise, the street was empty beneath the heat of the sun. The sky was high and open as heaven, but here on earth, it felt like hell. I was sweating, and my throat was parched. I was, as I had always been, between the carapace and the pit of flame.

The pedestrian took shape as I drew closer. It was the walker, in his brown UCLA sweatshirt. How could he stand to wear it in this weather? He was moving quickly as he always did, skirting the lip of the curb, hair like a halo or a nimbus. His mouth was clenched and twisted, although it did not appear to be an expression of pain or even sadness but rather one of rage.

"You," I thought I heard him say.

I had never seen him this animated. Talking to himself, shaking his head, gesticulating, as if he were in conversation. But with whom? I recognized the dilemma, or at least I thought I did. It was as if the axis of the world had shifted, leaving both of us adrift. The fire had unleashed something, or maybe it was the fire itself that had been unleashed. Either way, everything had changed.

I had never thought of him as mad, but then what did that say about me?

The walker stopped in my path and waited. We stared each other down from a span of six feet. Looking at his features was like gazing into a convex mirror; he looked like I might one day look, if I could survive. I recognized everything arrayed there: Corrina, Sylvia, my whole sad history. It was like coming face-to-face with the devil. It was like coming face-to-face with sin. He stared at me with fear and loathing. He stared at me as if he understood exactly what I'd done. His gaze narrowed as he watched me. He did not mean to let me pass.

I took a step, and then another. I could hear the ragged rhythm of his breath.

"Keep your distance," he said. "I see you. I see who you are."

Who was he and what did he want? What could

he possibly see? Just a crazy old man wandering the city, as if it were some biblical wilderness. Forty days and forty nights. And yet, he wasn't Jesus. We were both too old for that. In the yellow glare of the sunshine, his face appeared to darken, to grow a set of shadows that belonged to it alone. That nose, its beaky sharpness, and the high, hard cliff face of his brow. He wasn't the devil, I realized. More like a Dark Watcher caught out in the daylight, its powers diminished by the heat.

"I am the Lord thy God," he declaimed, "which have brought thee out of the land of Egypt, out of the house of bondage. Thou shalt have no other gods before me."

"Shut the fuck up," I told him. "What have you to do with me?"

The situation was absurd, or it was surreal. Quoting Bible verses as if he were a prophet or a deity. But what if? What if this were the secret of the universe? How much worse if God existed but was a madman, and this world a kind of disassociated fever dream. People wanted to imagine God, or its existence, as a source of consolation. I'd never bought into that, but what if the opposite were true?

What if there was a creator, and it was insane?

It would explain a lot, or it might, if you decided to believe it. It would explain the bitter and disrupted patterns of the world. The terror and the desolation and the loneliness, the beauty and the wonder and the love. Beauty was irrational also. So much so that often it hurt. And what was love if not despair in waiting? I had loved my wife but what did that add up to? I had given her everything and been laid bare.

I took another step, and the walker put up a hand.

"Stand back," he warned. "I don't want your contagion."

I was sweating from the heat or from the confrontation. It was difficult to breathe. For a moment, I wondered if I *was* coming down with something. Then I stepped into the street. It was like I was daring him to follow. It was like I was daring him to come along. But he just stood and watched, as if he already knew what I would do. I moved as quickly as I could to get around him, although it felt, still, as if I were under his control. What did I want? How could I answer? It was as if my agency had been stripped away. Only after I reached Cherokee did I start to come back to myself. I turned south there, towards Hollywood Boulevard.

And in the mind of the creator, who knew what might happen? This was the whole idea, that the universe was an improvisation, a set of serendipitous encounters, a narrative without a point. Or not without a point but without a purpose, even if you found yourself in the role of God. The most disturbing of ironies, that even the creator was at the mercy of the ebb and flow of existence, waiting to see, calculating the odds, working with scraps of information, creating the tattered fabric of the world out of loose ends, fragments, hallucinations — the moments, the half remembered bits of conversation it recorded and observed. Before I moved out of his sightline, I glanced back and saw the walker thumbing furiously on a cell phone, as if recording something he might otherwise forget. The story of our interaction, maybe, although who could say what that had been. Even the walker, I had to imagine, didn't know what he was typing. Even the walker didn't know where it would end.

The day felt like it had been going on forever. And yet, it wasn't even noon. Down on the Boulevard, people were everywhere. The sun was a broiler in the center of the sky. My eyes felt like glass and my head was full of sand.

Musso & Frank gleamed like an oasis in the semidesert light. I crossed the sidewalk, reached for the big green door, and slipped inside. It was air-conditioned and more than half empty as I took a seat at the bar.

"Maker's on the rocks," I said when the bartender asked for my poison. I felt better already, just sitting here. I was alone, and the air was crisp and clean, processed and purified and frozen. The low murmur of voices and the clink of cutlery offered a reassuring soundtrack. I was safe from the tumult of the street.

I avoided my reflection in the mirror as I waited for my round.

Back home, I was assaulted by the stench of the hummus. It stank like rotting human flesh. I shut the bedroom door to contain it, then for the first time in days opened the windows and breathed in the ozone smell of the afternoon. I left the curtains slightly parted — not enough for anyone to see inside, just to have a little light. Beneath the saturated glaze of the sun, I could see dust motes floating in the empty air of the universe like a million miniature satellites.

O God, I could be bounded in a nutshell and count myself a king of infinite space.

I switched on the music. It was the middle of the day and I didn't have to worry in the light. It was the darkness I feared and all the things that moved around within it. All the things that had left me unable to sleep or dream.

The speakers pulsed with the swampy echo of a Wurlitzer. A trio of chords repeated over low shuffling drums. I nodded along without thinking. Rolling Stones, "Just Wanna See His Face." The face, of course, belonged to Jesus, but that's not what the song meant to me. This was one of the records that had exposed me to blues and gospel, in what felt like a different century. Back then, I'd known nothing of the history. Back then, I'd only listened for the heat. Slow everything down so you could feel it, suspend the moment, stretch it, until it felt like time itself would explode.

Take this riff, this one loose riff, repeating for a minute before the falsetto of the vocal began to rise. At first, it was just syllables strung together. A form of primordial ooze. Mick Jagger repeating patter like the nonsense verses you might sing alone. Music as intimacy, as gesture, music as living, incomplete. I loved the song because it sounded so unfinished. I loved the song because it sounded so unformed. The same three-chord pattern until it turned hypnotic, coalescing into the repeating line of that refrain:

> *Don't want to walk or talk about Jesus,*
> *just wanna see his face*

It barely sounded like a song at all, more like the impression of one. A sketch finger-drawn across a pane of glass, watercolor smeared translucent until you weren't sure if you'd imagined or you had heard. Like a glimpse of something through a mirror darkly, blurred to incoherence the moment you looked at it head-on. The only way to approach this music was to sit with it, let it rise to fill the space around you, and just as quickly fall away. The only way to listen was to inhabit the silence underneath it, to recognize it as both negation and milieu.

What the hell was I thinking? I didn't know anymore. It had been a long day after an even longer night and I was in limbo, adrift in a world that refused to cohere. As the track faded, I strained to hear what it yielded, but nothing was there. On the coffee table, I saw the zip drive. I picked it up and rolled it in my palm. The song ended and a new one came on: Ry Cooder's cover of "Thirteen Question Method," Chuck Berry recast in the style of the Delta blues. Cooder had played with the Stones also. He had contributed those mandolin licks on "Love in Vain" when he was only twenty-one.

And love *was* in vain, wasn't it? Robert Johnson had understood that even before he'd written the song. I had never known a love that lasted. I had never known a love that survived. Not my wife and not Corrina. That had been no love at all. And what about the tulpa, who would be waiting always, even after she lost human form?

I took the zip drive to the bedroom. All the smells of birth and death were in there, the reek of new growth and decay. Give it a few days and mold would emerge, life in its most basic form. That was how I felt also, embryonic but at the same time about a minute away from giving up, walking outside again and into traffic, or jumping from a high place — a roof or outcropping — into oblivion.

I probed the wall around the tulpa's mouth with the tip of my finger. I scraped some of the hummus clean away. There were those lips, the clarion of their warning. They were saying things, or trying to, I couldn't hear. *No*, I thought or might have said out loud. *No*, perhaps I yelled. Then I mashed the zip drive through the tape and all the other mess, pressing it straight into the center of the wall.

In the living room, I flipped open my computer, scrolled the latest fire news. I was looking for an update on the body, a field note from the scene. I had no idea how the zip drive had gotten here. I had no idea what was going on. All I wanted was to slip into silence, to be one more anonymous soul in the city of the angels. All I wanted was to … evaporate. Was that so hard? It didn't seem too much to ask. And yet, here I was. One by one, I clicked through the news sites. But when I finally came across some information, it was not at all what I'd have wished to find.

The body, investigators were now revealing, belonged to a woman, and she did not appear to be a fire casualty. She had been there for some time. Months, perhaps, maybe years, no one knew for sure.

Long enough to have mummified.

I fell out of time again at that point. For how long I couldn't say. When I came back, I was in the bedroom, buried underneath the blankets.

I was screaming again.

QUESTION NUMBER TWELVE: WHEN WE'RE BY OURSELVES

The truth is it wasn't my wife who destroyed our marriage. I managed that all by myself. It happened long before our final flash of indiscretion. That was just the playing out. I didn't want to admit that it was all on me. That I had bullied and cajoled. I wanted to imagine that I was good. Or at least a sympathetic soul.

My wife had come to me like a figure from a fantasy. Like someone with no future and no past. I had imagined her as a cypher, a template for my desires. I had imagined that we would share everything. As to what this meant, I had no idea. I was so young, too. And damaged, each of us in our own way, complementary or otherwise. It was an astonishment that we held on for as long as we did.

The night with the other man, it was my idea, although I'm ashamed to say so. I had convinced myself it was what she wanted. It became easier the more she went along. We experimented with all sorts of role play. Increasingly as things fell apart. I wasn't working — I was never working — and she kept us afloat. This is why I didn't take anything when it was over, because none of it belonged to me. Just the money in the bank for the years together. And my anonymity.

My wife, I should say, had been game at first. Or at least that's what she said. She let me believe that she enjoyed it, all the things I am even now unwilling to reveal. It's better not to dwell on it. It's better not to say. That was the lie we shared at any rate, until we couldn't share it anymore. I was like Leopold von Sacher-Masoch, who forced his wife to be his dominatrix against her will. What does it mean that the man who gave masochism its name was always in control of the relationship? Perhaps only — or most essentially — that he was a man.

144

This is not a confession. I have nothing to confess. But it is ... let's say ... an acknowledgement — of how a marriage can slip out of hand in subtle increments, how the shared dream, or reverie, of intimacy, the ebb and flow of a relationship, can be consensual and coercive all at once. It cut both ways; she lorded it over me about the money, about my failures and my lapses in that regard. If she wasn't wrong, then who's to say about the rest of everything that happened?

Who's to say where the breaking point resides?

By that final night, when we went to Malibu, we both understood what was at stake. We both understood the problem, and that it could not be fixed. I remember her sitting silent while I drove the car, the same roads as when I'd crept out of the house and fled along the concrete rivers of the freeways, pushing the edges of my boundaries before something like a tether snapped me back. Those nights I'd spent mostly in silence, but for this ride, I had Huddie Ledbetter on the speaker, those walking bass lines and that deep tenor sounding like the voice of God.

> *My girl, my girl, don't lie to me*
> *Tell me where did you sleep last night*
> *In the pines, in the pines*
> *Where the sun don't ever shine*
> *I would shiver the whole night through*

We were in the car at my instigation. Everything else was done. Call it closure, a closing ceremony. Call it anything but what it was. I was not so good at waiting, although I had been patient enough. We drove west on the 10 and north on Pacific Coast Highway until we found the turnoff and wound our way up into the canyon, leaving everything we'd ever known, or thought we'd known, behind.

I lost time that night too. Or maybe I should say I lost myself. I don't recall what happened when we got there. I don't recall what happened when I left. I know we found some space in the clearing and lay down together, drinking from a bottle I had brought. Already, I had begun to find my refuge there.

My refuge and my release.

I wish it was as simple as those Leadbelly lyrics. But I knew where she was sleeping, not in the pines but in the bedroom, behind the door I'd shouldered open, insuring it would never fully shut or lock again. I remembered the look she gave me. At least I thought I did. A resigned shake of the head and a slow turn of her face towards the wall behind her pillows. I'd slunk back out to the living room, shame rising in my throat as thick as bile.

I don't want to give the wrong impression. I never raised a hand to her in the years we were together, even after everything went bad. She did not have the same restraint, although it didn't happen often, two or maybe three times, or was that the number of the blows? Once, I remember, we'd been on vacation, in a motel with thin walls; we'd had an argument and when I wouldn't keep my voice down as she pleaded, she struck me three times in the middle of my chest. It was like listening to a cock crow, an omen or a wakeup call. *Three times you will deny me*. In the morning, she apologized and I let it go.

But did I? Did I ever let it go or did I torment her, push her in all the ways I knew would cause discomfort and remorse? It was I who had insisted on the fantasies, and it was I who had made them three-dimensional, blurring the line between the imagined and the real. It was I who pressed her to drive to Malibu, and it was I who coaxed her to the clearing, with our car parked on the turnout up above. This was the same clearing where I would later leave Corrina, amid the dirt and brush, the fire rising. The same clearing where I would later leave myself.

And did I leave my wife there also? All I can say is that I never saw her again. As for the rest of it, I don't remember. It peels away from me like pieces of a dream. Did she even exist? Or did I invent her? I was good at conjuring illusions to fill in the gaps. Maybe she was just another spirit in two-and-a-half dimensions, a ghost, a Dark Watcher, some sort of specter. A tulpa let loose on the world.

But then, what about the body? Not the one that remained undiscovered but the one that had been mummified? It was a woman's body, the news sites were reporting, but other than that, details were scarce. No specifics on how long it might have been there. No specifics on when it might have been left. Or, for that matter, on what had happened. Cause of death remained a question mark.

Had I done something? What might I have done?

I trust you with my life, my wife had said to me, *but not with my body.*

Or had it been the other way around?

I rented a car on Craigslist and drove out to Malibu. Two hundred dollars in cash, which I paid using Sylvia's money. So much for evidence, I suppose.

I picked up the vehicle in Hollywood. A dusty little Honda Fit covered with dings. I couldn't decide if it made me more or less conspicuous. I didn't really have a choice. The car smelled stale, as if it didn't get used very often. But it worked and it was clean. I was near enough to where I'd left Corrina's car that I thought about making a quick drive-by. But I had already returned to the scene of one crime. Now I was returning to another one. A third would be too much, crow of the cock again. Beneath the flatness of the summer sky, I already felt exposed.

It was Saturday, or so the owner of the car informed me. Otherwise, I wouldn't have known. Time had become a flat circle, immovable and static, with each moment the same as every other one. The roads were full — convertibles with their tops down, SUVs full of parents and kids. Beach traffic, bound for Point Dume or Zuma or Leo Carrillo. It was the dark heart of the California dream.

I had never liked the beach, not in all the time I'd lived here. I had never once gone without duress. I hated the sand and all the people. It always left me feeling provoked. The only time I could tolerate the shore was in the evening, when the shadows lengthened and the bathers were gone. Like an ebb tide, draining people, instead of seawater. It was like watching the lights of the world go out. One day, it would happen to all of us. It wouldn't be dramatic, and no one would notice. It would be a matter of mechanics, a necessity of tidal flow.

With the traffic, I had to pay attention. With the traffic, I could not allow myself to drift. It didn't feel like freedom but rather obligation. The obligation to keep myself in line. Sometimes, behind the wheel, I would fantasize about what might happen. I would imagine veering into a different lane. The closest I ever came was to change lanes without looking closely, but even then I'd glance around a little first. I didn't want to die, or at least I didn't think so. I just wanted everything to stop. Not forever, but from this moment in the timeline. I wanted to go to sleep and wake up in some other moment, without a past, or at least without a memory.

The traffic continued to thicken as I drove further west. By the McClure Tunnel, it was at rush hour levels of stop-and-start. My windows were shut and the air conditioner was blasting. Even so, I began to sweat. I felt trapped in this little moving box in close proximity to all the other moving boxes.

Everyone was looking at me.

The PCH was no better. Long lines of cars waiting to turn left into parking lots that dead-ended against the emptiness of ocean and air. The sky was blue again, the fire pretty much extinguished, just a handful of hot spots here and there. As I moved north, into Malibu, I could see the evidence of what had been wrought. The fire had not jumped the road, that was one thing. The two-story brush along the coast remained as it had been. On the inland side, however, the hills were scorched black and denuded. This is where Cal Fire had made its stand. The firefighters had lit backfires wherever it was feasible; they had started a burn along this stretch of pavement to deprive the flames of fuel. Looking at it now, I felt a surge of ... pride? It was a little bit that way. I had done this, hadn't I? I thought back to those car fires, tried to trace a line from there to here. Fire was the devil's hand tool, but it was also how we clarified ourselves. Clarified and cleaned and prepared for what was coming. Its scouring was how we moved beyond the past. This was the story of Southern California, which was a wildfire ecology. That served as both fact and metaphor — like the phoenix rising from the ashes, a symbol and a crucible.

I rolled down the window and shut off the air conditioner. I could smell salt and also water, and beneath them both, an undernote of smoke. The beaches were full as I passed them. Only the scarred hillsides remained to remind us of how tenuous our place in such a landscape was.

At the canyon road, I took a right, and wound my way into the hills. I was surprised to see no cops, no checkpoints, even as the fire smell kept thickening. I could feel its tickle at the back of my throat. I inhaled and held my breath until I thought I would pass out. I wanted to draw the smoke not only into my lungs but also into my very cells. I wanted it to become a part of me. Everywhere I looked, the brush had burned away, all that wild rye, coyote bush, purple sage, and yarrow. Tenacious, yes, but not enough. Nothing could stand up to the flames. At uneven intervals, skeletal trunks of sycamore or eucalyptus rose up like gravestones. I remembered that there had been houses. I remembered seeing lights. But in the brightness of the afternoon, none of them were left. The news had said 100 million in damages. The number made Corrina's father's estate seem small. What was the phrase? Economies of scale. If nothing else, the fire had upped the stakes.

Up ahead, I could see the rhythmic flickering of police lights, a steady beat of red and blue. That meant I was coming to the place where the body had been found. I could see it in my head, the dirt turnout, and the slope leading down to where Corrina had been taken. But this wasn't Corrina, this was something different, and I still didn't understand what it meant.

I knew this road would lead me out the other end

to Mulholland or Topanga Canyon Boulevard. I knew that I had every right to take that route. All the same, it seemed dangerous. It seemed like tempting fate. Before I reached those police lights, I pulled onto the shoulder and began a three-point turn. For a moment, I thought about getting out and taking my place in the middle of the devastation, in the middle of everything I had caused. But I was too smart for that, wasn't I? It was enough that I had come. I still didn't have any answers. But it was the questions I didn't want to face. *What are you doing here? Seems a strange choice for a weekend drive.* So as those lights flashed in silence across the desecrated landscape, I finished my turn and set off in the other direction, the car fishtailing just a little, leaving loose tire tracks imprinted in the blackened dirt.

I didn't want to go home but I couldn't stay here. The car was mine for the afternoon. The day was an open question or the day was a blight. At the bottom of the canyon, I turned right and followed the coast road north. I drove through the Malibu Civic Center and up past Pepperdine, with its terraced lawns and the towering recessed cross that looked like a mold from which the true cross had been struck. It was impossible to imagine anyone being crucified there.

Once I got beyond the beaches, traffic thinned. I had no idea where I was going, but the movement made me feel free. Free, yes … and something else also, as if I were getting away. With every mile I drove further from Los Angeles. I got further from its vortex, from its pull. If I could just keep driving, maybe I would be all right. All the way past San Francisco to the Lost Coast. We had made a few trips like this, my wife and I, renting a cabin in Big Sur and continuing on to see the redwoods, where we opened our windows and breathed until we grew intoxicated by oxygen. It was the cleanest air I'd ever inhaled, and as it filled my lungs I felt not transformed but fully realized, as if this was how we were meant to live. You could take it one of two ways, I'd discovered. You could appreciate the moment, or you could lament that it had passed. I was more suited to the latter, but the oxygen in that redwood forest made me understand that I was a body, activated and aware. It was wonderful to be alive to feel it. I've gone looking for that feeling everywhere.

I stared at the coastline's rocky outline, the shore falling raggedly into the sea. The Pacific was blue and choppy white, wet-suited surfers bobbing in the waves. Across the road, brown hills and hidden canyons, as if no fire had ever occurred.

I didn't have to go back, did I? But no, the car did not belong to me.

A mile or so north of the Ventura County line, there was a roadside seafood stand. Weathered wood, a rambling shack of a place, parking lot half full with pick-ups and motorcycles mostly, locals on the way to or from the beach. Out on the front landing, a covey of patrons clustered at a row of short plywood counters, drinking beer and eating fish and chips off cardboard plates.

I hadn't realized I was hungry. It felt like I hadn't eaten anything in days. I slowed the car and turned in at the lot. Nobody looked at me when I stepped out. Over-head, a flock of seagulls. Their squawks sounded like muffled screams. I nodded aimlessly to myself, not mak-ing eye contact. I felt my chest loosen as I took a breath.

At the counter, I ordered a bowl of clam chowder. I ordered a bottle of beer. When I got my tray, I took it to the last plywood counter on the landing, where I could eat and drink without disturbance. Inside, a teenage boy was banging on an ancient video game; its hums and whirrs recalled another time. An hour northwest of the city, it was as if I had left Los Angeles behind.

I sat and sipped my beer, waiting for the chowder to cool. A wind had picked up off the ocean, and the air was growing misty, with the promise of encroaching fog. I could taste it as I began to spoon the chowder into my mouth. The mix of flavors was overwhelming: the clams, ocean-thick and briny, but also the garlic and the pepper and the potatoes. I had forgotten that food could be so ... sensual. I had forgotten the dimensionality of taste. I had forgotten that such a small thing could bring such pleasure. Or maybe it was pleasure itself — the possibility of pleasure — that I had overlooked.

I polished off the chowder almost without breathing. I ate as if I were a beast at trough. I finished my beer and got up to order another. I could sense the familiar loosening of the alcohol — a release, not a loss of control. I hadn't realized that I was ravenous. My body had been shaking, but I hadn't noticed until after I was done. Now, sitting at the counter as I finished the beer, I felt more than sated.

I felt as if I had been restored to life.

I went back to the city beneath a falling dusk, the sky purpling at the edges of the coast. Traffic picked up again as I drove south, and the smoky smell returned. It had been a reverie, another one: this idea of running away. Not just because of the car — that was all I needed, to get pulled over for grand theft auto — but even more the notion that I could escape to Mendocino or Yreka, maybe into Oregon. Even if I went all the way, straight down the line, I'd only end up in Alaska. And Alaska was nowhere I wanted to be.

No, I had found a place here. For better and for worse. And there was still unfinished business to attend to. There were still some things I had to do.

I returned the car and walked back through Hollywood along the nighttime weekend streets. Voices drifted from open windows in a chorus of cacophonies. I avoided any boulevard or intersection where I might find a crowd. It was a different kind of anonymity but when it worked it gave me cover. The question was how long that would last. I would have to make some sort of reckoning with Sylvia. I understood that she would not let me slide.

This was what I had let myself in for, I realized as I reached the court and unlocked my door. There was no place to run to because I didn't know what I was running from. Or, no — of course, I knew. I was running from myself. I had become my own mark in a con I didn't even know that I was playing.

I had no choice now but to see it through.

Inside, the rooms were dark and quiet. No ghosts, no tulpa, no memories. It was as if I had purged my own existence. I had the sense that were I to look in the mirror I might not see a reflection. Once again, I could not hear my footsteps as I crossed the floor. I kept the lights off as I hit the switch on the receiver, and music filled the room. The record was Jelly Roll Morton, "Don't You Leave Me Here." He had written it, or so he claimed, in the first years of the last century, although it was uncertain, really, whether he had written it at all. This was another thing I loved about the blues, that in so many cases, no one could pinpoint the origins of the songs. You could trace the history of the form, of the performers, but as for the individual pieces, so much was apocryphal. Even "Where Did You Sleep Last Night?" — had Leadbelly composed it? Yes, of course, in some sense, sure he had. At least, he had gathered it together. But the song had other roots, other versions. As for their authorship, that remained unknown.

I poured a glass of Maker's as Jelly Roll's barrel-house piano rose from the speaker. Then his voice, rich and textured, yet distanced, still, by the pressure points of time. He was asking someone — who was it? some long dead phantasm, a ghost or specter — not to disappear without making sure that he'd been cared for, without giving him a dime for beer.

A dime, yes. Or that array of hundred dollar bills that I'd collected. I sipped the whiskey as I gathered everything for one more look. There was the money, minus what I'd spent on the Craigslist rental. There was the 5150 intake form. I checked to make sure the curtains were drawn before I switched on a light. I checked to make sure the windows were closed. I spread everything across the surface of the coffee table and I opened the laptop, sitting for a moment in its empty glow.

The news sites had no additional information. Just more reporting on the damages and the ongoing investigation of the body, which remained unidentified. I wanted details, a description maybe. How old she was, or how long she'd been there. I wanted the details to exonerate what I could not remember. I wanted them to set me free. But I had been free, just a few hours ago, hadn't I? I had been free until I returned. What this told me was that freedom was a lie, a false promise, although that was something I already understood. How could you be free when the clock was ticking? How could you be free when time would always take its toll?

I picked up the intake form again: an argument, a fight, the threat of violence. That had been Corrina's way. She had commandeered me, that was the only description that made sense, from the very first night she'd come here. Still, there was something I was missing, something about the connection between her and Sylvia. The money, the sequencing of the bills, it was more than a coincidence. There was more at work than merely Sylvia paying her in cash.

What had she said? I tried to think back to our conversations. I tried to make sense of it all. She had mocked Corrina, that was one thing, although she had also turned a mocking eye on me. But that wasn't the essential point. No, it was more that she had understood her, known her well enough to predict what she might do. *Have you come home to find her in your bed?* is what she had asked me. And then I'd come home to discover precisely that. It was as if they'd been through all of this together. It was as if it were something they had shared. How did she call it so exactly? I felt it then, the cold rush of … not adrenaline, exactly, but revulsion, a shock that felt an awful lot like dread.

I finished my drink and poured myself another. Sylvia's voice was in my head. She had told me about the 5150s. She had told me about the two rehabs. She had explained the cash, the payments from the estate. I had found out about the apartment, but that was hardly a surprise. Rich kid, with a father who had always bailed her out. I could imagine him pretending to be tough, threatening that each time was the last time, when all along, they both knew it wasn't true. He had bought the building, for fuck's sake, so she wouldn't have to worry about being evicted, so she would always have a place to live. Was that the nature of their relationship? A quid pro quo, a mercenary dynamic. What was required of her in return? Corrina had said there was something more, but Corrina said a lot of things. Sylvia too. *Sometimes she does a little job for me.* It was hard to imagine what those commissions might have been. A website, a portfolio, a family photo …

All of a sudden, I thought I understood.

I opened a browser on the laptop, and opened the fetish site. As I searched for the images, my eyes fell across others, far more graphic: Catherine wheels and bondage, backs and buttocks flayed until they bled. What I saw on those screens made me wonder, one more time, about the desire to be seen. Maybe it wasn't shame but self-expression. Maybe these people were proud of who they were. Maybe if I'd been more like that, it would have been better. Maybe I wouldn't have had to keep so much from view. That decision, though … it had been made so long ago that it didn't feel like a decision. It felt like part of who I was.

I found the photos and scrolled through them. I was looking for the shadow of the shooter, that was all. The curve of an ankle or a shoulder. Anything that might uncover who she was. She? Yes, because I was pretty sure now, because I was finally starting to understand. Somewhere in the middle distance lay the answer. Somewhere in there lay the key. Somewhere between the shade and light, the past and present, was the last piece of the puzzle. Somewhere, all would be revealed.

And yet, for a moment, I was distracted. For a moment, I found myself deterred. For the first time, I noticed — or thought I did — Sylvia's face as she swung the whip. Behind the mask I could sense a sadness. Or maybe coercion is a better word. Either way, it was like watching a façade slip, like seeing the situation plain. I had thought of her as the driver. I had thought of her as the relentless one. But looking at her now, she seemed less ferocious than

155

reluctant.

Not for the first time, I was reminded of my wife.

I don't know how long it was until I saw it, but I had been leaning over the screen for quite some time. The night was dark and the music had gone quiet. I had no idea how late it was. Then, in the middle of the sequence, I noticed, or thought I did, a detail I imagined that I must have missed. The father bound and gagged, Sylvia behind him. And in the corner of the frame, not a shadow, not exactly. Something more like a mistake. There it was, or there it seemed to be: the tip of a low boot on what must have been the shooter's foot. It was a brown ankle boot, not unlike what Corrina had been wearing the evening I met her, and most of the evenings after that.

I felt myself grow queasy. I wanted to throw up. I quit out of the site, then reconsidered. What if I were the one who'd been mistaken? What would I see if I clicked the link again? But I couldn't take another look. All of that to lead to this, and what did any of it mean? I finished my drink and stalked into the bedroom, my chest feeling like it might explode. It reeked in here, of rotten food and body funk, of all I'd wanted and could never have. The tulpa remained obscured, for the most part, by the hummus, which had thickened with mold and crust. The zip drive leered at me like a wet tongue from out of that plaster mouth of broken teeth.

"What the fuck?" I said, voice trembling. "And you think I'm the crazy one?"

Then I drove my fist into the wall, once, twice, three times, as my wife had once done, long ago, to me. I felt the plastic of the zip drive splinter, and a fragment — or was that metal? — pierce my skin. When I drew my hand away, I could see a sheet of blood across my knuckles. Another smear shone red on the wall.

I had been played. From the very beginning. It had all been a put-on.

Now it was up to me to set it right.

QUESTION NUMBER THIRTEEN:
HOW CAN I BE CERTAIN?

My knuckles weren't scabbing. I had scraped them raw. They glared back at me from the backside of my hand like a face that had been beaten open. I went into the bathroom and ran them underneath the tap. The cold water cut like icy blades. It was not refreshing, it was another assault. Everywhere I turned, assaults on my reason, assaults on my propriety. And all because I hadn't seen what was right before me. All because I'd allowed myself to be fooled.

That photo, for example. How many times had I stared at it? But apparently, I had missed the larger picture. Poring over the center of the image, rather than the edge. That had always been my problem, the inability to recognize the trees for the forest. As usual, I had fallen prey to my desire.

And what was it I wanted? Even now, I couldn't say. To belong? I had never belonged, although it did not make much difference to me. To be seen? If anything, it was the opposite. I had spent so long trying to remain *un*-seen. It was easier that way, or safer. It created a necessary buffer of raw space. I didn't want to be *seen*, I wanted to see, to recognize the terms for what they were. *The world is a bucket of shit,* someone had once told me. Although I no longer recalled the circumstance, I recognized it as a fundamental truth.

And yet, I hadn't seen, had I? I hadn't seen a fucking thing. All this taking place right in front of me, and it was as if I were in a novel or a play. Going through the motions, pretending to be in control, when I was at the mercy of a puppet master, Sylvia or Corrina or I didn't know who else. The tulpa, a malevolent creator scripting such a drama. The idea of it enraged me. I slammed my fist against the sink.

And opened again the cuts across my knuckles, the blood as red and pulsing as my rage.

In the living room, I swallowed down a glass of Maker's. Then I went to the shower and turned on the spray. I felt my muscles loosen under the hot water, which turned pink as it washed across my hand and spiraled down the drain. I was going to have to go up there. I was going to have to make some noise. I was already imagining the confrontation, Sylvia in that big empty house, coming to the door in the middle of the night and finding me on the other side of it, full of righteous anger. It felt like I'd been gearing up for this for my entire life.

If I was heading up the hill, I needed to be presentable. I needed to play this to the hilt. I got out of the shower and shaved and combed my hair back. Then I put on my blue suit and my red tie. I knotted the tie carefully in the bathroom mirror, my best approximation of a Windsor knot. Above the knot, the face I saw was unfamiliar, pale and thin. My eyes were rheumy, striated with a latticework of small red broken vessels. They looked like raw eggs. Corrina's scratches had faded pretty much completely; afterimages were all that were left. I raised a finger, ran it along the line of one. Under my touch, the skin felt new and tender, paper thin.

In the living room, I turned on music. I needed some distance if this was going to work. Out of the speakers, Elmore James again, singing "Dust My Broom." I listened to his slide guitar, that sweet and piercing sound, a sound I didn't know that I would hear again. That, and the low gruff whisper of his voice.

I believe my time ain't long

As the music rose behind me, I gathered up the evidence: the 5150 intake form, the sheaf of hundred dollar bills. I retrieved the smashed-up zip drive from the bedroom, where it remained implanted in the wall. As I pulled it out, I thought I heard a cry of pain.

"No more from you," I said.

I wasn't sure if I was talking to the tulpa or if I was talking to myself.

I had another drink and went into the kitchen. I looked in the utility drawer until I found the lighter I had bought when I moved in. I weighed it in my fingers for a moment. I could hear the fluid slosh within. I put it in my pocket and picked up the money and the other items. Then I stepped outside.

The courtyard was dark and midnight dreary. I could smell jasmine, and mixed within it, a whiff of garbage and concrete. Summer in Hollywood, when everything swells like an infection, until it ripens and bursts and spreads its disease.

Corrina's place was still open. I mounted the steps and picked up the hibachi, which I carried inside. I needed to be careful; I didn't want ash or charcoal on my clothing. It wouldn't do to show up at Sylvia's with traces on my suit. In the darkness of the living room, I removed the lid from the hibachi. The briquettes remained within. I wondered if they'd ignite or if that time had passed. It was too late to do anything about it either way. I set the hibachi in the middle of the living room and layered in the intake form and all the money. Hopefully that would get the fire going, or keep it from going out. I was not trying to burn down Corrina's bungalow, just trying to make a statement. Like those car fires … I didn't want to hurt anyone.

And had I? Had I hurt anyone, even now? It was impossible to say. What was the line between Corrina and Sylvia? Had Corrina ever truly lived at all? Maybe she had been a fragment of my imagination. Mine, or Sylvia's. Or both. The Malibu fire was extinguished and there was no body … or at least no body that had belonged to her. Without a body, how could anyone have killed her? Without a body, there was nothing anyone could say. And now there was, or would be, no evidence.

I took the zip drive from my pocket and tossed it on the grill.

The lighter torched when I struck the flint. I touched it to the intake form. On the other side of the hibachi, I sparked a hundred dollar bill. The paper caught at the edges and began to smolder before it burst into flame. I lit a second, and a third.

The conflagration came on slowly. One more element taking me by surprise. The coals had been sitting for a long time, but I watched as they started to ignite.

This was the barbecue Corrina had wanted. This was her fantasia brought to life. I felt myself choke up at the thought of it, at what I had been able to provide her, even though she was gone. The flames rose out of the middle of the grate. Their flickering lit up all the walls. I could make out shadows, and what looked like faces: Corrina, Sylvia, my wife. They danced in the flames as if this were a holy invocation, as if this were a Dionysian rite.

I knew better than to stay in the apartment. I could smell the burning paper, the melting plastic of the drive. I would carry those odors with me when I left here. I could not escape their trace. As for what else I would carry, I didn't have anything left. The hibachi was too hot to move. It was time for me to go.

I tossed the lighter on the burning pyre and passed through the door back out into the shadows. I was almost to my place when I heard the lighter explode.

Inside, I poured a drink and picked at the scabbing on my hands. In the bathroom mirror, I looked more wan, if that was possible. It was as if my soul had been sucked out. Behind me, the flames kept rising inside Corrina's window. I couldn't tell if they had spread. Some men just want to watch the world burn. I touched my chin, my cheeks, and pressed the new skin. I sunk my nails in and I tore.

The pain was one more rite of passage. The pain reminded me of what it meant to be alive. After I was finished, I had reopened all the wounds. My face was scoured with blood. I glanced at my knuckles, my stigmata. It looked like I had been revealed.

In the living room, the stereo was playing. "Dust My Broom" again; I must have put it on repeat. My time ain't long, my time ain't long … well, it was time now,

160

wasn't it? The clock was ticking, as they say. I picked up the bottle of Maker's. I took a drink and poured the rest out on the floor. Another ritual, another rite of passage, a way to commemorate the dead. But who was I mourning? My wife, Corrina, all of us. Or maybe just myself. I felt weightless, as if my body had dissolved.

Outside, I took a look at Corrina's apartment. No one appeared to have noticed the fire. I lingered on my step and drew a deep breath. Then, I locked the door behind me for the last time and turned my back on it all.

It was a straight shot from Hollywood to Benedict Canyon. All I had to do was walk west. First on Franklin and later down to Sunset. Just another lost angel in the city of night.

The Magic Castle was lit up above me on the hillside. It glittered in the dark like a mirage. It was late, but the club stayed open until two. I knew because I had been there once. In this suit — there was a dress code — accompanying my wife on a business perk. Some out-of-town client had wanted to see it, and so a member's invitation was procured. I didn't usually accompany my wife on work outings; it was as if she didn't want her associates to know about me. This was the one time: *It'll be fun*, she'd said, in a tone a lot like pleading. It was only when we got there and I met the other spouses that I understood.

This was how the marriage had worked, each of us exploiting, or framing, the other, not a relationship or a conversation so much as mutual use. It was a matter of what we wanted, a matter of how much we could take. I made small talk and smiled nicely. We ate dinner with her associates in one of the club's dining rooms. Then we saw a show and visited the music room, where a ghostly piano player took requests. I had just started my retreat into the bottle; I remember paying attention that night so I would not drink too much. I had no idea that I would one day end up here.

Now, the castle seemed to me like a reminder …

or maybe more than that, a haunted house. It wasn't that it had meant anything to us, but we had been there. We had moved through its labyrinthine corridors together, or at least in the same time and place. Now, I lived in its shadow and almost never thought about it. It was mostly part of the scenery. But tonight, I could feel it. I could sense the flickering echo of that other life. It wasn't anything I wanted any longer, or anything I thought I could have. It was just another broken promise, another haunting. It was just another lie.

I followed Franklin until it dead-ended at Sierra Bonita. Then, I cut south to Hollywood. Here, the boulevard was as quiet as a side street, two lanes in each direction and a line of low apartment complexes, three and four storeys tall. The sidewalk was narrow and it was empty, beneath a tall row of Mexican date palms. These were the trees everybody thought about when they thought about Los Angeles, with their ridiculously skinny trunks and towering crowns. They were part of the look of the place, but the irony was that they were transplants, like so many of the rest of us. This was the burden of Los Angeles, or maybe its great gift. In a city this sprawling and uncentered, certain images were required, certain clichés, to allow people to think they could get a grasp on it. But the secret of Los Angeles was that you had to give that up to understand it, or at least to recognize it on its own terms. It was a city like all the others because it was a city unlike all the others. Its meaning *was* its chaos. That, I had discovered, was the whole idea.

This stretch of Hollywood was an example. It had nothing to do with the tourists. There were no landmarks, no Walk of Fame, no celebrity impersonators. Just another nondescript residential neighborhood, the kind you might find anywhere. And those palm trees? Blackish at their branches, stained by carbon monoxide, crusted trunks choked with dust and sand. Urban trees that didn't even belong here, that had been brought over and implanted from somewhere else. As I passed beneath them, I felt a certain kinship. As with me, no one saw them any longer.

As with me, it was as if they were no longer here.

And was I? Was I even present? I was all alone. Walking, after midnight, through streets not meant for the pedestrian, despite their sidewalks and their curbs. To walk at night was a way of removing yourself from the city. It was a way of coming face-to-face with the emptiness of these unpopulated thoroughfares. It was city as apocalypse. It was like living through a pandemic and realizing you were the only person left. Or no, not the only one because you had vanished too.

Normally, I would have felt edgy, alone at night, moving through these neighborhoods where I did not have a place. Normally, I would have been concerned about the possibility of confrontation in my suit and my red tie. But I no longer cared about that. What could anyone do to me? With my face, I imagined I was frightening. I imagined I was a figure to be avoided, endowed with extraordinary force.

At Crescent Heights, I turned onto Sunset, emerging at the eastern edge of the Strip. There were people here, tourists coming out of the comedy clubs or wandering to the Chateau Marmont. I tried to keep my distance, to stay away from the places where they might cluster. But there were too many lights. I heard gasps, some laughter. The more jaded, or affected, tried to pretend everything was cool.

"Hey, man," a voice called from in front of the Comedy Store. "What happened to your face?" It was a male voice, young, and it provoked a chorus of responses, from what I assumed to be its friends. I wandered over. A group of teenagers stood in front of the door. I could feel them shrivel as I drew close.

I said: "Don't make me do the same to yours."

The force of it, the power. I could feel it coursing through my limbs. All those years, letting things happen, and now it was on my terms. The group of boys in front of me stood their ground for half a second, then turned and scurried away. I looked around, as if seeking another challenge. But nobody was willing to look at me.

I passed the Whisky and the Roxy. I noticed everything, as if seeing it for the final time. On the other side of Doheny, I left the glow of the Strip and entered the long low sweeping part of Sunset, the Boulevard of myth and memory. Enormous estates behind vast walls of shrubbery and gates on either side of a broad and curving avenue. The quiet was so thick it felt as if sound itself no longer existed. There was no one on the street. It was in one of these houses that *Sunset Boulevard* had been set, that movie narrated by a dead man, everything in retrospect. It felt so close to me that I could almost touch it, almost imagine myself in his shoes. I remembered the end of the film, after the narrator had been murdered and Norma Desmond, that great lost star of the silent era, was about to be taken away. She had lost her grip on reality and decided it was all a script. *All right, Mr. DeMille, I'm ready for my close-up*, she announced as the police waited. Until this moment she had been entirely forgotten. It had been as if she were already dead.

I was not forgotten. How could I be, when I had never once been known? But everything was about to be different. All that was about to change.

The air felt cool and liquid. It was what I liked about Southern California summer nights. After dark in the semi-desert things grew dense and fragrant, the day's heat little more than a memory. I'd been walking now for well over an hour; I could see the lights of the Beverly Hills Hotel ahead. There were cars parked in the long circular driveway and, in the background, a low hum of music and conversation. That meant it was not yet two. I remembered the last time I had stopped there, to get a Lyft after leaving Sylvia's. I had sat in the Polo Lounge and ordered a Maker's. Now, I was back again. My throat was parched and my head hurt. I could have used another drink. Maybe when I got to Sylvia's. Maybe I'd talk myself indoors and sit in that study with a full glass while she and I had it out.

I passed the hotel and turned north on Benedict Canyon, steeling myself for the ascent. It was a steep street, winding, and although it was too late for a lot of traffic, I knew I'd have to keep to the shoulder if I didn't want to run the risk of being hit. I could feel the pressure build in my lungs as I started the climb. My lungs and the back of my calves. Each step was like pushing on a bicycle, like trying to coax my body into doing something it didn't want to do.

And then, on that terraced street that twisted above Sunset, I glimpsed something irrefutable. The night was dark and silent. The houses that rose along both sides of the macadam were shuttered and still. The last time I'd been here was when the fire was raging. Everyone had been panicked and forlorn. But now that reality had snapped back into place, the illusion of invulnerability had been restored, the sensation that everything around me was protected and apart.

And yet, the city remained its own construction, an imposition on the natural world. This, too, was something I had always liked about Los Angeles, those incursions of the elemental, whether in the form of fires, floods, and earthquakes, or in the wildlife that made its home around the edges, or in the corners that maintained proximity to the wild. Even in Hollywood, you could see it: scorpions or spiders, the rattlesnakes in Griffith Park. It was a reminder that the universe could bite you. It was a reminder that the universe was wild. People came to Southern California for the dream of ease, but it was the undomesticated nature of the territory that exhilarated me the most.

That was what I was seeing now: the city, or the landscape, as it really was, as it would be when all the human beings were gone. Walking down the middle of the canyon road, in a single-file progression that appeared to hew to the yellow center line, was a pack of coyotes, seven or eight of them, their noses long and lupine, their fur a mix of gray and brown. All were adults except perhaps the last one, which looked smaller than the rest. I stopped and receded to the foliage. It wasn't that I was scared. I just didn't want to reveal myself. The coyotes didn't look at me, although surely they must have known that I was there. Instead, they kept a steady pace and formation, like a military unit on patrol.

I took shallow breaths as I watched them. I didn't want to make a sound. For the first time, I became aware of a light fog in the night air. As the pack continued down the hill, the focus faded. The coyotes grew indistinct and blurred into the mist. This was no illusion either. This was just the way of the world. It was night in California and the wild things were out. And no one to observe them but a Dark Watcher, traversing the nocturnal quiet of the hills.

I stood there until I couldn't see them any longer. I stood there until they were out of view. Then I started again, continuing uphill. The coyotes had been silent but not in any otherworldly sense. More in the sense that a predator is always quiet as it stalks. That was what had given them such power. That was what had given them such grace. Nothing ghostly or ethereal about it. Just the essence of the real.

Well, I was real now also. And I was closing in.

Ahead, through the haze and the darkness, I could make out the entrance to Sylvia's driveway. I could picture its circular flow in my mind. The fountain in the middle, and the courtyard, and the gravel and the slate. I stopped to gather myself before I set foot on her property. I stopped to catch my breath. It must have been past two now. It was as if the whole city was asleep.

The first thing I did was to case the joint. I checked the windows and the doors. Everything was sealed up tight. This was as I had expected. Not a seam to facilitate the incursion of the outside world.

Now that I was here, I had all the time I wanted. But time had ceased to be of use to me. All of it, every second, every minute, leading to this moment. I mounted the front steps and pounded on the door.

I don't know what I expected. It was hard to know with Sylvia what she wanted, what she was willing, or not willing, to give. In the past, she had left me hanging. In the past, she had made me wait. Not this time, however.

Maybe it was the hour or maybe the urgency of my fist against that portal, but it didn't take more than a few seconds before the lights inside the house began switching on.

And those lights, they were confusing. They were coming from too many sources at once. Upstairs, downstairs, a variety of windows. But how could that be if she were alone? From inside, I could hear footsteps. They seemed to be going in more than one direction, to the front and to the back.

What the hell? I thought.

And then the front door opened, and a young man in a buzz cut, wearing black jeans and a black tee shirt, filled the space in front of me.

"Can I help you?' he said simply. His body was immense.

"I'm here to see Sylvia," I told him in a voice that sounded full of dust.

"It's 2:30 in the morning. What business could you have with her?"

"Who are you?" I asked.

Before he could answer, I sensed the presence of someone else behind me, and felt a pair of hands encircling my wrists.

"Look," I said, but he didn't want to hear it.

"You're trespassing," he said.

In the house, I could hear Sylvia's voice low and urgent, as if talking on the phone. I couldn't make out the words but I had an idea what she was doing, with whom she was speaking. I could imagine her in that den, calling the authorities.

"It's okay," I said, "It's my mistake."

The pressure tightened on my wrists.

"It's too late for that," the young man said and he hit me, fist a solid shape connecting with my solar plexus. I didn't remember anything for a while.

When the world came back, I was face down on the gravel, the little stones cutting new channels in my face. My wrists were fastened behind me with what felt

167

like a zip tie, and it hurt to draw a breath. I craned my head and saw Sylvia in the doorway, wearing a kimono. She was talking to two men. One was the guy who had hit me. The other must have been the one who'd held me for the punch.

"What do you want us to do with him, Mrs. Glenn?" the first was asking. I couldn't hear what she said in response. Then, the men came to where I was lying and roughly pulled me upright. It hurt too much to stand, so I crumpled to my knees. That was where I was when Sylvia came down the steps to greet me, a petitioner in my suit and tie. Saturday night, Sunday morning. I knelt as if I were in church. This had started on a Saturday, hadn't it? It was hard to remember. It felt like so long ago.

From low in the canyon, I could hear the sound of sirens. Was there any question what they were? It wouldn't take long before they got here. It wouldn't take long before I was out of time.

"Sylvia," I said, my voice a raspy supplication.

She looked down at me as if we had never met.

"I'm sorry," she said. "Can I help you?"

"I know everything," I said.

Her face was a closed book, giving nothing away.

"I know about the photographs," I continued. I could feel myself cascading, speeding through the words. In the canyon, the sirens grew louder. It sounded as if there were more than one. "I know about the building, about Corrina and her father. I understand about the money—"

She cut me off with a harsh laugh. "I don't know who you are or what you think you're doing. But I can assure you that you don't know a fucking thing."

Don't know who you are? The words were like another fist. They doubled me over with fear and doubt. How was that possible, unless ... I didn't want to think about it, I didn't want to know. Sylvia was leaning toward me, those clean white teeth as sharp as chunks of plaster in the middle of a broken wall.

"But here is what you're going to know," she continued. "I'm going inside now, and my housemen will keep an eye on you until the police arrive."

I didn't know what I was thinking. I didn't know what I should do. I didn't know how I had misread everything. I didn't know how I had gotten it so wrong. Of course, Sylvia had housemen. How could she live in a house, a neighborhood like that and not? Maybe they'd been here the whole time, as I had imagined, waiting to be needed. Maybe they had been waiting for me since the beginning of time.

But this had been my time, hadn't it? At least that's what I'd believed. My whole life spent living in the shadows and this my moment to be seen. The sirens kept rising. It sounded as if they were almost here. Along the edges of the night, I could see the flash of red and blue lights. They were coming here for me.

For me, yes, the flashing lights were coming. It was my moment, after all.

I knelt in the darkness and I waited.

There were just the sirens and I shone.

About the Author

David L. Ulin is the author or editor of nearly 20 books, including *Sidewalking: Coming to Terms with Los Angeles*, shortlisted for the PEN/Diamonstein-Spielvogel Award for the Art of the Essay, and the novel *Ear to the Ground*. His fiction has appeared in *Black Clock, The Santa Monica Review, Scoundrel Time,* and *Zyzzyva,* among other publications. The recipient of fellowships from the Guggenheim Foundation, the Lannan Foundation, and Ucross Foundation, he is the books editor of *Alta Journal,* and a Professor of English at the University of Southern California, where he edits the literary magazine *Air/Light*.

9 781944 853907